I0710315

# SMALL COCKPITS AND BIG HANGARS

PETER SCHUTES

ADAM MAXWELL BIGGLESWORTH

*Do you love to fly? These four sexy stories will make you fasten your seat belt and reach for your oxygen mask!*

## THE PILOT AND THE PUPIL

When high school senior Willie Best gets bumped up to first class, he meets Bradley, a pilot with a very big package to deliver. From the bathroom to the cockpit and hotel penthouses to dirty basements, they discover earthly delights with sky-high endings.

## MILES HIGH

Jeffrey hates to fly. When his porn star seatmate discovers his little secret, the panic turns to passion in the airplane toilet.

## CHOPPER JOCK

Rudy Acker, the helicopter pilot for the local news, has had nothing but rejection and bad luck in bed. His giant curse becomes a blessing as he meets the kind of men who can handle his needs. He finds love in the unlikeliest of places.

## DUTCH TREAT

An airline captain tries to take a snooze at the hotel inside the Amsterdam Airport but meets up with a giant Texan who has anything but sleep in mind.

# CONTENTS

## THE PILOT AND THE PUPIL



## MILES HIGH



## CHOPPER JOCK



## DUTCH TREAT

Small Cockpits and Big Hangars
Copyright © 2024 by Peter Schutes Publishing.
First Edition © 2024
All Rights Reserved.

ISBN: 978-1-963667-11-0

No part of this publication may be reproduced, distributed, or transmitted in any form or by any means, including photocopying, recording, or other electronic or mechanical methods, without the publisher's prior written permission, except as permitted by U.S. copyright law.

The story, all names, characters, and incidents portrayed in this production are fictitious. No identification with actual persons (living or deceased), places, buildings, and products is intended or should be inferred.

Cover Illustration by Kate Woods-Chisholm

This book is for ADULT AUDIENCES ONLY. It contains substantial sexually explicit scenes with multiple partners and graphic language which may be considered offensive by some readers.

All sexual activity in this work is consensual and all sexually active characters are 18 years of age or older.

# THE PILOT AND THE PUPIL

by Peter Schutes

# FIRST CLASS

My name is Willie Best. When I was eighteen, I flew back to Seattle from my coed boarding school on the East Coast. I looked a lot younger than eighteen back then. I had a delayed onset of puberty, so I didn't have pubic hair yet. My penis was very small, too, because it had never received the benefits of testosterone. I never got the growth spurt, so I was below average height, too. Throughout my teenage years, I felt ashamed of my tiny, hairless penis, my short stature, my plump man boobs, and my skinny body. The girls didn't seem to mind hanging out with a boy who looked twelve, but the guys were mean. They called me "baby boy" and pushed me around a lot. I was too petite and skinny to fight back, and I began to enjoy the negative attention. My sex drive was intense, puberty or not.

All that attention from boys made me realize I was not into girls, at least not sexually. I pictured my itty bitty penis, maybe an inch hard, not quite reaching their vagina. In the showers, where the boys called me "inchworm," "titty boy," or "wee

Willie Winkie," I marveled at the variety of penises. None were as small as mine, but plenty of little guys were in those showers. What really got me hard, though, were the boys with the big, dangling schlongs. I was too naive to know why or what I could do with them, but I was excited to see boys with man-sized cocks soaping up. A few of them looked at me funny, but I never had a clue what they wanted. I was still a virgin when I got on board that flight to Seattle.

I had to go to a holiday party at home, so I planned to pack my sport coat, tie, and a Brooks Brothers button-down shirt. I realized they would get wrinkled in my tiny bag, and the best way to keep them fresh was to wear them on the flight. I looked like a little boy at his first communion or bar mitzvah.

Logan Airport was a madhouse that Christmas. There were canceled flights, lost bags, and outraged passengers everywhere. My cab took thirty minutes just to get me to the curb. I sprinted to the gate, my small suitcase in tow. When I got to the podium, the woman behind the desk smiled at me.

"Oh, little boy, are you lost?"

I hated when adults mistook me for a little boy, at least until that flight. I said, in my most resounding voice, "I'm eighteen. Here's my driver's license."

The woman blushed. "Sorry, sir, but you look adorable in that suit, and I just thought...oh, please forgive me."

I nodded. "No problem."

She said, "We're fully booked for this flight, and I'm afraid we don't have a seat for you. But..." She consulted her clipboard. "Oh, I see we do have a vacant seat in first class. Would you like to sit there?"

I was a scholarship student. I'd never flown business class, let alone first class. I wondered what it would be like.

"Yeah, of course. That would be awesome."

She smiled and handed me my boarding pass. "You get to board first."

The loudspeaker squeaked. "Flight AA16 to Seattle is now boarding at gate 13. First-class passengers are invited to board now."

I was in a sea of wealthy grownups, several of whom smiled down at me, clearly mistaking me for a youngster.

I sat in the luxurious seat, only four to a row instead of eight like the back of the plane. The seat reclined. I was in a window seat, no wing blocking my view. I gazed at the busy workers in the icy wind, loading bags and driving little carts to and fro.

When I tore myself away from the window, it was just in time to see my seatmate taking the aisle chair. He was dressed like an airplane captain. His tight polyester pants clung to his legs like stockings. Down his left leg, I couldn't help but see the outline of a massive cock. It strained against the fabric as he placed his bag in the overhead bin. I couldn't see his face, and I stared unabashedly at the larger-than-life penis. It was soft, but it reached halfway down his thigh. I wondered if it got any bigger when it was hard.

I'd heard a little bit about gay sex by then, but I had never so much as jacked off with another guy. It was only six years after Stonewall, and nobody knew much about gays other than a fellow who threw a pie in Anita Bryant's face. So looking at a colossal cock turned me on, but I had no reference point for why or what it meant other than the fact that I was gay.

The man closed the overhead bin and sat next to me, adjusting his cock, which had slipped under his thigh. I forgot to stop staring.

"What you looking at little boy?" Coming from this gruff man with a full mustache and model good looks, those words made my little dick throb.

"Um, nothing, sir. I mean, you're a big man."

The pilot blushed. "Yeah, I am."

I liked his face. "You're a pilot; don't you fly the plane?"

He chuckled. "Nah, I'm deadheading back to Seattle, son. I've got a flight to Tokyo the day after tomorrow."

He put his hand on his thigh, gently adjusting his cock out from under his legs with the palm of his hand. I tried to look away, but my eyes kept darting to the fat roll of flesh under those pants. The pilot watched my eyes, studying me like a slide under a microscope.

"What's your name, kid?"

"Willie."

"I'm Bradley."

He extended a paw, and my hand disappeared inside it like he was holding a small flashlight.

"Your hands are so tiny."

I hated my little hands, but I felt sort of proud because of the way he said it.

"You going home for the holidays?"

I said, "Yeah, I'm at Buxhall Academy. It's break time."

"You're in high school?"

What year are you?

"I'm a senior. Just turned eighteen."

He continued nudging his cock under his polyester pant leg. I could see it throb and grow. I was hypnotized. He turned and caught me staring.

"You like what you see?"

It was bold and strange coming from a grown man of at least thirty. I shifted uncomfortably in my seat. My tiny pecker was poking at the fly of my chinos. I doubted he could tell.

"Um, it's really big."

We were interrupted by an announcement from the cockpit.

"This is your Captain speaking. We're delayed while we wait for the snowplow to clear the runway. We've been assured we'll be third in line once we get the all-clear in about 45 minutes. Until then, I'm gonna turn off the seatbelt signs, and you can smoke if you're seated in the last eight rows."

The stewardess appeared with a cart. She smiled at Bradley.

"Hey, Brad. Good to see you."

"Yeah, you too, Donna."

She added one ice cube and emptied a tiny bottle of whiskey into a big glass.

"Make it a double. I'm not flying for a spell."

She opened another bottle and filled the big glass to the rim, setting it down.

"What about you, young man? What can I get you to drink?"

I was old enough to order booze, but I decided against it.

"Can I have apple juice?"

As soon as Donna pushed the cart to the next

row, Bradley's hand was back on his cock. Now, it was all five fingers and his palm. He rolled it gently from side to side like he was rolling out dough for biscuits. It swelled and stretched toward his knee.

"You want a sip?"

He passed the whisky over to me. Damn, this guy was into me! I took a sip of the fiery, cheap airline liquor.

"Aw, come on, have some more."

I took a big gulp, then coughed and spluttered.

Bradley chuckled. "One more."

I took another big swig. This time, it went down easy. I felt that dizzy warmth come over me.

Bradley smiled at me, and I melted. "Kid, you probably never felt anything like that, huh?

I'd had a few drinks at the school play after parties, and I knew how good it felt to catch a buzz.

"No, sir." I liked telling lies to this man.

Bradley's left hand never left his thigh. He pinched and rubbed it, turning the stretchy polyester squares into diamonds.

He leaned over and whispered in my ear. "You a faggot, kid?"

I shook my head, lying.

"You look like a little faggot to me, boy. You like my dick, don't you?"

His mustache tickled my ear, raising the sparse, downy hair on my arms.

I had never felt so thrilled and terrified at the same time. I nodded.

"Have you ever seen one this big before?"

"No, sir." I wasn't lying.

"Your dad got one like mine?"

I shook my head. Dad was just average, maybe a

little smaller. When he was soft, it was just a little wrinkle of skin, then a head. I saw him hard in the shower once. It was a grower. I must have inherited my tiny pecker from someone else.

Donna came back up the aisle with her cart. Bradley pinched her ass. She slapped his hand away, grinning.

"Can you slide me another? Double."

She sighed and took his glass, adding an ice cube and two bottles of the bitter brew.

"I got this for you. You like it?"

I shrugged. "It feels good after."

Bradley's lips turned up at the corners. "You like feeling good, don't you?"

He took my tiny hand and put it in his lap, covering it with an in-flight magazine.

"Go ahead, feel it good."

I was stunned. My hand barely covered the width of the massive beast in his pants. I felt it pulsing and straining as I gave it a good squeeze.

"Yeah, like that. You like it?"

I gave an enthusiastic nod.

He leaned in and whispered again, tickling my ears with that sexy mustache. "You want to see the whole thing?"

"Yeah."

His volume dropped. "I'm going to that bathroom. I'm not gonna lock it. Wait a few minutes, then you meet me there. I'll let you watch me piss. You dig?"

I nodded. Bradley stood up, walking stiffly to the front of the plane. He closed the bathroom door.

I counted to 300, then I teetered and wobbled to the restroom. The whisky had removed my inhibitions and sense of balance. The door was unlocked. I pushed it, watching it fold. Behind the door, I glimpse Bradley with his pants around his ankles. I could only see the first three inches of his colossal cock. He grabbed my hand and pulled me in, snapping the lock shut.

I stared in disbelief. The pilot's cock was rock hard, pulsing, standing so tall he would only need to bend his neck, and it would have gone right in his mouth.

He tousled my hair.

"Good boy. Oh, put your hands around it."

I couldn't touch my fingers with one hand, so I used two. I had no clue as to what he wanted next.

"Oh god, those tiny hands make it look even bigger. Put your cheek on it."

I leaned forward, rubbing my cheek against the huge beast. The vein running along the underside was thick. I could feel the blood coursing through it as it pressed against my cheek.

"Willie, I know I promised you I'd let you watch me pee, but I can't. My cock is too hard. I need your help."

I had only the slightest notion of what he needed, but I was ready to do anything for this man.

"Uh, how can I help?" My virginity stank.

He picked me up and sat me on the sink so my face was at the same level as his cock head.

"Can you put your mouth on it? It's not dirty."

I encircled the end of the shaft and pulled the head toward my mouth. It was so hard, I had to really tug. He had the kind of penis I'd seen a few times in the showers. It was fat, but the head was pretty small. It got very thick in the middle, then a bit thinner at the base. I was able to get the whole head in my mouth. I licked the tip. It tasted salty. The whisky went to my head. I felt giddy.

"That's it. Good boy. Don't let your teeth touch it. I want you to keep doing that."

While I was sucking on him, he unbuckled my belt, then unbuttoned my pants. He roughly grabbed the waistband of my pants and underwear and pulled them down.

"Oh fuck, it's so little." He said it with deep appreciation. "Such a fucking beautiful little dick."

Instead of shame, I felt a rush of pride fill my head. He liked my little hairless dick. I felt him cover it with one fat finger, wiggling it back and forth.

"Damn! That's a fucking little dick. You can't do shit with that dick. Can you even jack off?"

"Yeah, but it just feels like I gotta pee, so I don't do it much."

He frowned. "You don't shoot yet?"

I still had never ejaculated. My delayed puberty had fucked me over on that front, too.

I asked, "What's it like when you shoot?"

He said, "I'm gonna show you. Now get your mouth back on my dick."

I slurped on the end of his dick like it was a melting ice cream cone. He put his hands behind my head, and I felt him push me down. I slobbered and sucked as the end of his dick found its way to the back of my throat. I gagged. He stopped.

Hold it there, son. Just let it pass. I choked, retched, and gagged until something slippery from deep in my belly came up. It smelled like puke. It made me gag more. He grabbed a tissue and wiped the end of his dick clean, dabbing my face. I liked the attention. And I loved choking down his cock. It made me feel sexy.

"Good boy. You're ready."

With a violent shove, he pushed his way past my tonsils. My lips stretched too wide; I could feel them starting to tear. I tried to back off, but he held me there, gagging and struggling. I loved it, but it was hard work.

"Come on, little bitch, you can handle it. Your little clit is wet." His dirty talk made me feel like I was being bullied, and it turned me on.

I touched my penis, and it dripped like I'd peed, but it was clear and sticky. I was so aroused, I guess it flipped a switch somewhere. Was that cum? I thought it was supposed to be thick and goopy. Maybe this was all my body could muster. But I hadn't felt that throbbing sensation yet.

Touching myself took my mind off the assault on my mouth. In fractions of an inch, Bradley shoved more of his cock in my throat. I couldn't breathe. I flailed my arms, wondering if this guy would choke me with his dick of death. I wasn't ready to die. I started punching him in the arm. He relaxed and let me up.

He slapped me playfully. It made my cock throb. It reminded me of those bullies at school, the ones with big cocks and fists, pummeling me after school. How I'd wished those boys would have held me down and forced me to suck their cocks. I finally got my wish, even if the bully was nearly twice my age.

Bradley held my ears, bobbing my head up and down, his cock head sliding deep past my tonsils, then back out. It felt so good to suck a cock. I moaned.

"You like that, son?"

I tried to nod but couldn't. "Mmhmm."

"Yeah, you do. Little faggot."

I'd been called that name more times than I could remember. It never sounded sweeter coming out of the mouth of this grown man.

An announcement came over the loudspeaker. "This is your Captain. We're clear for takeoff. Please return to your seats." The fasten seat belts sign lit up in the bathroom.

"Oh, shit. Faster!"

The bathroom went blurry as he forced me up and down jackrabbit fast. I couldn't gag, it was so fast. And it felt like my throat was going to come. It throbbed and contracted.

"Oh yeah, you little slut. You're having a throat-gasm. Fuck! That feels so good!"

The waves of pleasure traveled from my throat to my crotch. Bradley pinched one of my tits hard.

"You got bitch tits. You're practically a girl. It's fucking hot."

The abusive words were music to my ears. I stopped touching my wet penis because it was throbbing in that way right before I dry-orgasmed. I was too close. I was too late.

My tiny penis reared back and, to my surprise, spouted its first load of cum. It got all over the base of Bradley's cock.

"You little fucker. I'll bet that's your first time! Get ready for mine."

He used my cum as lube and stroked up and

down his shaft, hitting my chin before plunging back to his bushy pubes.

"Oh fuck, I'm close. Keep sucking."

I was moving on my own now. My pilot had both hands on his cock, practically punching me in the jaw on each upstroke. I was afraid I would bite him.

"Get ready. Get ready. Ohhhh!" He let go of his cock and used both hands to force my head further down his cock than ever before. A warm blast filled my throat. He let go of my head, and I instinctively backed up, feeling the goopy cum splatter my tonsils, then my tongue. He pulled out and shot the last of it on my face.

"You're a good little faggot, aren't you?"

I nodded.

"You made me proud. You liked that a lot, didn't you?"

I smiled and shrugged.

"You're gonna be a dirty cocksucker. You'll be busy, son."

As he talked dirty to me, he wiped the cum off my face. I licked some like frosting.

"Oh, you're a filthy cum eater, you little whore. I'm going to fuck you silly when you're broken in enough to handle it."

I watched, fascinated, as he coiled his cock into a ring before straightening it out down the left leg of those shiny polyester stretch pants. I hiked mine up quickly and buckled the belt. A wet spot appeared on the fabric where his cock ended. I wanted to lick it, but he pulled the door and shoved me, so I fell on the floor."

He stepped out and said, "Hey, guy, did I knock

you down? You're supposed to be in your seat. Come on."

I followed him back to our seat, where he played with his cock during takeoff.

"Can I have your phone number?"

I was glad he asked. "Of course."

"You live in Seattle?"

"I live there in the summer and in Boston the rest of the time."

"Parents divorced?"

I shook my head. "I live at school."

"Oh, you're one of those rich kids flying first class."

"I'm a scholarship student."

He grinned. "Right on."

The plane leveled off, and the seat belt sign went off.

"Do your parents know you're a faggot?"

"No," I said.

"Give me your number in Seattle. I want to see you again. You'd like that, right?

He was so into me. "Sure, I would!"

"Yeah, little buddy. And then we can do that again. You liked it, right?"

I nodded.

"You're really good at blow jobs."

It certainly felt like work, so I could see why they called it a "job." I didn't remember blowing much. Was I supposed to blow on it? I doubted it.

"Thank you, sir."

He grabbed his cock through his pants. "God, you fucking turn me on when you call me 'sir.'"

I looked out the window. Through the clouds, I could see pastures and fences dotting the landscape.

Donna brought a chicken dinner that didn't taste like cardboard. The gravy was full of capers, which I had only just learned to like. Bradley gave me his pudding.

"You earned it. Besides, I'm cutting down. Gotta keep this body lean."

He made a muscle.

"Feel that."

I put my hands around his bicep, but they couldn't touch.

"Almost as big as my dick, right?"

I laughed. "It's bigger, sir."

# 2

# COCK PIT

After they cleared our trays, Bradley leaned in to whisper again. I would never tire of that tickle from his mustache. I got shivers.

"Hey kid, have you ever been in the cockpit of a plane?"

I shook my head. "Nuh-uh."

He gave a mischievous grin. "You wanna meet the Captain and the Co-Pilot?"

I did. I was about to meet the Captain! It was exciting.

"I gotta tell you, though, they're a lot like me. They like being with young men like you. You up for that?"

"Are they as big as you?"

Bradley pulled back and laughed. "Nobody is. Nobody, kid."

He wrapped an arm around Donna's waist as she passed. "You got the key to the cockpit. I wanna show this kid how they fly the plane."

Donna smiled and escorted us to the front of the plane. She rapped her knuckles hard on the door to the cockpit, then opened it.

"Captain, are you up for a couple of visitors?"

The Captain was older than Bradley. He had piercing blue eyes and grey at the temples. I smelled his Vitalis aftershave. It was the smell of men. Big, burly men.

"Who do we have here?" When he smiled, the corners of his eyes wrinkled.

Bradley said, "This here's Willie. Don't worry, he's eighteen, but never been fucked."

The Captain extended his hand. "Captain Paul Harris. But you can call me Poppa." His hands weren't as big as Bradley's, but they were rough and hairy, covered with freckles.

The copilot licked his lips. He was young, maybe in his mid-twenties. He reached over and punched my cheek gently with his knuckles. His hair was that shade of red that looked brown.

"Hey, little man. How's it going? I'm Eric."

The door to the cockpit slammed shut. Donna was gone. The tone of the room shifted.

Bradley said, "I got a live one. You guys gotta break him in. I wanna fuck him so bad."

They didn't even pretend to show me the controls. They must have been on autopilot because they stood up and surrounded me like jackals.

The captain's crotch rubbed against my tummy. I felt a big chunk of meat in there.

Eric, the copilot, cleared his throat. "I suppose you want me to go first."

Captain Harris snorted. "Fuck yeah. We gotta break him in."

Eric pulled me to his crotch. "Unzip me, faggot."

I pulled the zipper down.

"Pull it out."

I reached in. It was a thin, average-length cock. He was already hard.

"Suck on it."

Sucking his much smaller cock was a relief after Bradley. I put the whole thing in my mouth and pressed until the tip hit my tonsils. That was as far as Eric could go.

"Damn, you got small hands! Put your little hands on my ass and squeeze it."

I obeyed. His butt muscles were perky. It felt good. He let me suck him for a long time. I could see Bradley and the captain stroking their crotches. The captain's was much more prominent now. It jutted out, straining against the fly of his pants. He pushed it down until it went partway down his leg, and then he just squeezed it.

"Hey, pay attention!" Eric smacked me hard. "Stop being a little bitch!"

I felt my cheek burn. I didn't know why the painful slap made me hard again, but it did. Not that anyone could tell. My dick was so small and insignificant.

Eric said, "You ever get fucked before?"

I shook my head.

"Keep it in your mouth!" He smacked me again. I grabbed his hand and held it against my cheek.

"Oh, you like that, huh?" He struck me. I nearly saw stars. He was a bully too. It made me wet.

Captain Harris said, "Lay off! We need him conscious when he goes back to his seat." He picked up a bottle of Corn Huskers Lotion and tossed it to Eric.

Eric pulled me off his dick roughly and applied the goopy wet slime to his cock. "Stroke it."

I put my hand on his cock. My fingers touched. The head was thicker than the shaft, the opposite of Bradley's. It was uncircumcised, which looked strange to me. All the boys at my school were cut, and so was I.

"Oh fuck, those little hands make it bigger."

I didn't mind Eric belittling me. I felt like I was part of a club. I didn't know for sure what 'getting fucked' meant. I'd heard rumors, but they didn't make sense. Poop came out of there. It was one way. Could something go in?

I got my answer when Eric put a cold, slippery finger on the edge of my butthole. He pressed firmly, and the finger slipped inside. He went deep, right up to the knuckle. It hurt pretty bad.

"Oh, your little virgin ass feels so sweet, Willie. Not a hair in sight." Eric tried to work a second finger in me, but I yelped in pain.

He smacked me on my cheek.

"Quit crying. I'll give you something to cry about in a minute!"

I relaxed, submitting to Eric's digital assault. I felt something new once the second finger was in, and the pain subsided a little. There was a button in there, and every time his knuckle pressed it, my dick tingled. The feeling spread to my balls and then my stomach. I was tingling.

"You like my fingers in your pussy, don't you?"

I hadn't heard my ass referred to as a pussy before, which confused me for a second, then everything made sense. It was a hole for a dick to go in.

Eric fingerbanged me until my little cock started to dribble more of that clear juice.

The cockpit radio came to life. Captain Harris

cursed under his breath and took his seat, answering the call with letters, numbers, and a lot of aviation jargon I didn't understand.

Then Eric put in the third finger. I cried out in pain. The captain whipped around and said, "For fuck's sake, keep it down!"

I tried to stifle my cries, and it mostly worked. Eric chuckled as his knuckles pushed past my tight hole. He leaned forward and whispered in my ear. "Ready or not, here I come!"

I felt the large head press against my tight little hole. Eric clamped a hand over my mouth. With the other, he held the shaft of his cock while he pressed into me. I wriggled off. He smacked the back of my head but said nothing. The captain was still on the horn with some radio operator somewhere. We all had to be quiet.

Again, Eric positioned his cock head on my hole and pressed. This time, it slipped partway in. It didn't feel too bad. Yet.

In one rapid motion, he grabbed the front of my waist and held me still while he popped the head inside me. The edges of my vision turned red. It hurt so bad, but his hand held my mouth closed, so I had to scream out of my nose.

He hissed in my ear, "Shut the fuck up, you'll get us all in trouble."

Even though he was rough, I still liked being the focus of all his attention. It felt powerful. The waves of pain pulsed with decreasing frequency. Then, the pain just vanished. It was like I hadn't felt it. Instead, I felt an electric current running between Eric's dick and my asshole. That's the only way to describe it.

He was connected to me, and I was connected to him.

"If I let go of your mouth, are you gonna scream?"

I shook my head.

"Okay, then." He released my mouth and grabbed hold of my waist to keep me still. He stood behind me, his pants puddled at his ankles, and waited. I rested against the back of Eric's unoccupied seat. My butthole hugged his cock, waiting for him to do more. He pushed until his hips were against my flat little butt. I felt the thick head slide over that little button. It was better than ice cream.

The captain finished his radio dialogue and stood up. I could see the outline of a very thick cock throbbing in his pants. He put a hand on it and watched as Eric began to hump me.

"How is it?"

Eric said, "Oh man, not a hair anywhere. He's so smooth. And this tight little virgin ass..."

Bradley said, "He likes it, don't you, buddy?"

I nodded.

Captain Harris said, "You'll get your turn, Brad. We got an order we gotta go in. Let Eric finish warming him up."

It didn't take a genius to guess what they were up to. Eric's little dick would give way to whatever monster Captain Harris had in his pants. And then, it seemed, Bradley would kill me with his dick of death.

The cockpit was a tight space, but there was room for all of us. I watched Bradley and the Captain massage their cocks through the fabric while Eric took his fill of my ass. I didn't know why, but I wanted it to hurt more than it did. The electric pulse I'd felt when he first popped inside me was just a static spark now. I liked how the fat little head made me feel as it pushed my button, but it wasn't enough.

"You like that, boy?"

I lied. "Yeah."

I wanted to move on to the next challenge. This was getting too easy. I'd loved choking on Bradley's colossal cock. It was as fat as my little arm and longer than my whole head. Eric was nothing in comparison. I was bored, even when he picked up the pace and started to do it rough.

"Take it, you little bitch!" Over and over, his hips slapped my buttcheeks. That felt good, but it wasn't rough enough.

"Harder." I knew I shouldn't have said anything.

Bradley and the Captain both laughed at Eric, who smacked my ass harder than I'd ever been slapped before.

"Shut the fuck up, you little whore! It ain't hard enough? Take this!"

He held me around the middle and fucked me like a playing card in the spokes of a bicycle. His breathing grew shallow, and then he stopped suddenly.

"Ohhh! Yeah!" I felt his warm cum bubbling inside me. And then he was out. He pushed me off of him. My mind reeled. I didn't like Eric, but I loved how that made me feel.

Captain Harris spoke. "It's time for Poppa. You hold that seed up in your hole cuz you're gonna need it when I get in there."

I clenched my stretched hole, keeping Eric's jizz up inside my ass.

"Help me with these." The captain unbuttoned his trousers and loosened his belt. I knelt before him, hooking my fingers over the waist, and pulled. Slowly, the pants struggled against the engorged cock and muscular legs. As I pulled, I saw the thick base of Captain Harris's cock pressed hard against his big balls. As the pants came down, they revealed more and more of the fat beast. Another inch and his cock snapped out, striking me on the chin. I jumped back.

The captain chuckled. "It's not as scary as Brad's. Why'd you jump?"

What was scary was the girth. His shaft wasn't as thick as Bradley's, but the head was much, much thicker. It looked brutal.

"Come to Poppa." The captain sat in his seat, waiting for me to join him. I stood beside him, staring at his thick piece of meat.

"Do you need me to suck it, sir?"

"Call me poppa. No, I just need you to help me slick it up."

He handed me the bottle of Corn Huskers Lotion. I put a blob in my little hand and spread it on his cock. He jumped at the cold. I braced for a smack, but none came.

"Oh! That's cold, son. Keep rubbing, it'll get warmer."

His kindness contrasted with Eric's abusive manner. I liked this man better. A lot better.

"Like this, Poppa?"

"Yeah, that's good, son. Perfect."

He closed his eyes and sat back. I added more cold lotion to my palms and rubbed them together to warm it up. He didn't jump when I put it on.

"That's my boy. He's a smart one, a quick learner."

"Thank you, Poppa."

Captain Harris smiled at me. "Poppa's gonna have you sit in his lap pretty soon. Let me see that tight little butt."

I turned around and bent over so he could see my hole. He spread the cheeks and put his whiskers up to my butt. Then I felt his tongue lap at my hole.

"Eric, did you have garlic yesterday?" He chuckled. Eric grunted, ignoring the remark.

The captain returned to licking my butthole. He held my waist and pushed in, letting his tongue work its way into the crack. It felt great.

He said, "You like when Poppa licks your hole?"

"Yeah."

He turned me around and looked at my tiny, throbbing penis.

"Christ, it's so small. Do you want me to make it feel good?"

I nodded.

He put his mouth over my mouse-sized cock and balls and nursed them like a nipple. I shivered. It felt good, but I was embarrassed they were so small. I felt like I had disappointed Poppa.

Then he said, "Maybe one day, it will all get bigger."

I groaned inwardly. I was eighteen. My dick was never going to grow.

The captain said, "Okay, son, put your feet on the seat there, either side of my lap, yeah?"

I stepped up so my crotch was right in his face. But he didn't lick or suck me. He held my waist.

"Let your legs go loose, son, like you want to sit down. That's it."

He held me aloft as my legs went slack. His arms were powerful. I could see the tan muscles under his white shirt; they were thick, just like the rest of him. He dangled me over his cock until I felt the head slide between my cheeks and bump up against my butthole.

"Son, I don't want to, but I'm going to have to hurt you. Is that okay?"

I said, "Yes."

"Yes, what?"

"Yes, Poppa. You can hurt me."

He smiled. "I promise it will only hurt for a few minutes. You think you can take it?"

I nodded.

He let gravity do a lot of the work. It hurt. I tried to catch my footing so I could push back. Poppa scolded me.

"Son, don't fight it. Just let it happen. Wrap your legs around my waist."

I obeyed. My ass caught fire when the head started to move a little deeper. I cried out in pain, but the captain just held me still and let the pain subside before pushing another half inch deeper. His cock head flared wider than Bradley's shaft. It was the one place he was bigger. I didn't think I would survive another half inch of that long, fat head, but the captain just kept lowering me and pausing, lowering and pausing, until, at last, I felt a painful pop, and my ass snapped shut around the shaft below.

The next minute was sheer bliss. The wide head slid deeper inside me, pressing against that button, giving me chills. The captain lowered me faster until I felt the broad head press against the end of my rectum. Then he picked me up, so his cock pulled out until my tight hole trapped the head. He lifted me quickly. The colossal cock head popped out with a searing rush of pain. Before I could cry out, he sat me back down hard. The pain redoubled, but the wide head pushed the button, and it became a wonderful mixture of pleasure and pain. I felt my little dick leaking again.

The captain saw and smiled. "Oh, you like it. You like when Poppa puts his dick in your ass."

I nodded.

He bounced me up and down, each time popping out and back in, overwhelming me with pain and ecstasy in equal measure. My cock was drooling like a snotty kid with a cold. It got on the captain's tie. He didn't mind.

"Poppa's making you feel good, huh?"

I nodded. A wave of pleasure overtook the pain. Nothing hurt now. That electricity I had felt with Eric was nothing compared to the spasms of joy in my butt.

"Poppa's gonna hurt you one more time, and then it'll be good. You ready for it?"

I nodded.

He tilted me to the right, then let me drop. I felt a horrible pain on my left side as he tore past something. I saw stars, then the lights went out.

When I revived, the captain held me to his chest, buried inside me. I saw a bloody paper towel on top of the trash.

"Did you poke a hole in me, Poppa?"

He chuckled. "Not exactly. I went through a hole that was already there. Does it hurt?"

I shrugged. I wasn't sure. It felt weird having something big and fat stuffed in my butt so far that I couldn't even fart. I felt like I needed to.

"Poppa, I gotta cut the cheese."

Bradley and Eric joined the captain in a long, loud laugh. "Go ahead, son."

I tried, but I was plugged up. I wriggled and felt Captain Harris's huge cock head slide deeper. Suddenly, there was room for air to escape. It came out in a high-pitched whine, whistling between my hole and the skin of the enormous cock. It felt so good I shivered.

I was seated entirely in the captain's lap. His crotch hairs tickled my bottom.

"Okay, son. Are you ready for Poppa to fuck your hole?"

The words were so dirty. I liked it. "Yeah, Poppa, fuck me. Fuck my pussy."

He grew stern. "It's your hole, not your pussy. You're not a girl."

I was confused. Eric had just called it a pussy.

"Sorry, Poppa."

He stood, buried inside me. I held on to his waist with my legs. He laid me down so I was lying flat across the two jump seats. He grabbed my ankles and held them aloft, looking down to see his fat cock going into my tight, slim ass.

"This is how I like to do it. Missionary. Goddamn, that's a sweet hole, son. Cherry sweet."

I looked between my legs as he pulled back. His thick shaft looked surreal coming out of me. I could see a bit of dried blood along its length.

"I'm sorry I bled on you."

The captain leaned forward and kissed me, putting his tongue in my mouth. "I don't mind, son. I'm sorry Poppa hurt you."

"It doesn't hurt anymore."

He winked. "Good. Here comes the good part."

And it was incredible. Poppa first took short strokes, forcing himself in and out of that inner hole. As I stopped jumping, he took longer strokes. That thick, fat head slid over the magic button. His rhythm was gentle and steady. Each time he pushed the button, the waves of pleasure grew stronger. Then, they went out of control. I spasmed. My whole lower digestive tract was throbbing and contracting on its own.

"Oh, yes. We got a squeezer!" The captain looked up at Bradley, who made the thumbs-up sign.

"What's happening?" I was barely able to speak.

"You got an ass orgasm. It's giving Poppa a squeeze job, son. Oh, you make your poppa proud!"

I bucked and squirmed, unable to stop the waves of muscle from tightening around the captain's colossal cock. My eyes fluttered, and I groaned.

The captain concentrated on keeping a steady rhythm. It was that constant, rhythmic pushing that kept the "ass orgasm" going. Eric had been focused on how I could meet his needs when he fucked me. The captain was all about me and my pleasure.

The captain ran a rough hand up under my button-down shirt and over one of my fleshy tits. He swirled the nipple around, sending a new wave of sensory information into the mix. My little pee-pee got really hard, and then it spat out a load of cum on my chest and chin. It was only my second time ever, and it was twice as much as the first.

"Poppa's boy is spunky."

I tried to smile, but my mouth wouldn't cooperate. The quivers, shivers, and shakes were out of control. I thrashed back and forth, hitting my head against the cabin wall.

"You're gonna make Poppa come!"

I wanted him to. My arms flailed as I twisted from side to side, my moans climbing into an ever-higher pitch as the captain fucked me so deliberately that the vibrations in my gut just got more and more intense.

He pressed hard. His whole head popped into my colon and let another gust of air out. I felt intense relief when the fart blasted out of my ass past his thick cock. And then I felt a warm flood in my gut. It gurgled and spat, basting my insides with the captain's baby batter. He collapsed on top of me, breathing in that same calm, rhythmic manner with which he'd fucked me. I looked into his eyes. He kissed me, holding my head tightly. His fat tongue filled my mouth. His breath passed into my mouth and down my windpipe. Then he breathed mine for himself. I put my tiny hands on his beard and stroked the sideburns.

"Your Poppa loves you," he said.

"And I love my Poppa."

Eric cleared his throat. "Captain, it's time to begin our descent."

I looked at Bradley, who shook his head.

"Isn't it your turn?"

He smiled. "Tomorrow. I'll get you that hamburger and we can spend some time in my hotel room. I can't do it here. There isn't enough room." I had to agree. The cockpit was a tight space for four men.

The captain took the PA mic in his hand. "Ladies and gentlemen, this is your captain speaking..."

# 3

# IN MY SEAT

Back in our seats, Bradley lifted the armrest and got a blanket from the overhead bin. We shared it. He pulled me close and then reached his hand down the back of my pants. Nobody could see as he fingered me. I was so loose after my fucking that he was able to get three fingers in before I squirmed. On the fourth one, I let out a whimper. He stretched his fingers apart. Some gas escaped, but it was silent.

"You won't hear your farts for a while." He smiled at me. His face was perfectly symmetrical, and a small scar below his eye made him perfectly imperfect. He could have been a movie star if he had ever given up his pilot career. His thumb found its way in. Then he pressed forward, trying to get his knuckles past my hole.

"Push out like you're trying to poop."

I obeyed. His whole hand slid inside me on a slippery trail of cum and Corn Huskers Lotion. He left it inside my hole the rest of the flight, pressing my joy button until a wet spot developed on my chinos.

I couldn't see it because of the blanket, but I knew it was there.

Bradley took my little hand and placed it on the rock-hard lump that stretched down his pant leg.

"Squeeze it."

It was amazing that he had enough blood to get hard. Me, I only needed a few drops, and my tiny dick was stiff as a board. He probably needed a whole quart. When no one was looking, he planted his mouth just below my collar and sucked hard enough to leave a hickey.

"I've marked you now. You're mine. Can you tell your parents that you're going out with a friend tomorrow?

I nodded. "Yes, sir."

"I dig it when you call me sir. Especially when my fist is crammed up your sloppy wet asshole. You're a good little faggot. So fuckable. You love getting fucked, don't you?"

"Yeah."

The plane made a hard landing, jamming Bradley's hand deeper into my hole. It felt great.

When the fasten seat belt sign turned off, Bradley made a giant fist and pulled it out of my ass, practically turning me inside out.

"Ow!"

Nobody heard me over the sound of people grabbing their luggage and waiting to deplane. When he pulled out his fist, it was just slightly bloody. He wiped it on the blanket and smiled. He had my number and my address. When we walked off the plane, he pretended not to know me. When my parents rushed forward to hug me, he was already gone. I limped as we walked to the parking lot.

My mother asked, "Willie, are you hurt?"
I smiled. "I stepped funny in gym class."
"Would you like to see a doctor?"
"No, Mom. I'm good."

# 4

# OUR FIRST DATE

The next day, I was scared and excited, waiting for Bradley to call. I stayed close to the phone, waiting to pick up. I had a bad case of puppy love. It rang.

As luck would have it, my sister answered.

"Willie? It's for you."

Bradley breathed hard into the phone. "You ready to hang out?"

"Yeah," I whispered, "I'll meet you on the corner."

I gave him my address.

"Mom, I'm gonna go hang out downtown with a friend."

My mom said, "Are you sure? They say it's gonna rain. Don't catch a cold! Take your Mackinac."

I buttoned up and limped out into the cool Seattle fog. My ass was throbbing from yesterday's brutal beating, but it felt like a victory. I wasn't a virgin anymore. I waited at the corner. Bradley pulled up in a rented Olds Cutlass Supreme. He rolled down the electric passenger-side window.

"Hop in, kid. Let's go get some burgers."

We didn't get burgers or even go to Pike Place Market because I said, "Can't we fuck instead?"

"Oh, damn, you're a little whore! A little cunt-ass whore. I hit the fuckin' jackpot!"

We drove out to SeaTac Airport, where Bradley had a room at the Holiday Inn. I'd never been to a Holiday Inn. They had an indoor swimming pool off the lobby, which smelled of chlorine and Pine Sol.

"I'm up on the fifth floor."

A woman in a wheelchair rolled into the elevator and said, "Two, please." I poked the button for both floors.

Bradley stood behind her as we rode to floor two. He quietly squeezed the monster in his pants. I thought about how it was going to feel when he invaded my shitter with that giant fuck stick. I thought Captain Harris was hung like a horse. Bradley was a fucking elephant. I gasped as his pants stretched and strained against the giant cock running down his left leg. The flesh churned beneath the fabric as he rubbed it.

The elevator dinged, and the door opened. The handicapped woman rolled forward. "Thank you, son." If she only knew what Bradley was about to do to me, she might have a stroke.

For the three-floor journey, Bradley held me tight against him, humping my leg. He kissed my forehead.

"Don't be scared. I know how to make it feel good."

I nodded, no less scared than before.

We both limped down the hall to Bradley's room. I limped because my ass hurt, Bradley because his cock was stiff down that left pant leg. He had trouble bending his knee, as if his cock were a splint.

Inside his room, Bradley tossed me onto the bed like a rag doll.

"Take off your clothes." He watched as I obeyed. I hesitated when I was down to my socks and BVDs. My young body looked so tiny and frail in the closet door mirror.

Bradley unbuttoned his dress shirt, revealing a broad, hairy chest. He stripped off his undershirt. I knew he had muscles but hadn't realized how big they were. Everything about him was big.

Bradley needed my help getting his pants off. I knelt before him, unbuckling his belt. Then I un-snapped his pants, lowering the zipper. A few pubic hairs poked out; he wasn't wearing underwear.

As if he'd read my mind, he said, "They don't make any in my size."

I tugged, revealing the base of his cock. Even though I'd seen it already, it seemed much bigger than I remembered. I gulped, thinking about that thick tool stretching my hole open. It was too big, like it'd rip me in two.

I continued to drag his pants over his butt, tug-ging at the legs as they started to bunch and gather around his cock. The pressure of the huge, swollen monster made it more difficult as I tugged down. It was like a lever, strongest at the end.

With a sudden spring, his cock broke loose and smacked me hard on the chin before whizzing sky-ward past my ears.

He kicked off his pants and pulled me to my feet.

"Get it good and wet."

I had to stand back to take the monstrous head

in my mouth. It was so long I didn't need to kneel; I just stood hunched over a bit. The corners of my lips still chafed from yesterday, but I ignored the stinging pain and pushed until the head hit my tonsils.

Bradley grabbed my hair and pumped me up and down, each time digging a little deeper into my throat.

I coughed, gagged, and spit up. The bile smell made me retch over and over until spit was coming out of my nose and rolling down his shaft.

"Yeah, boy, that's the best lube there is." He jacked his cock with the slimy spit-up. I retched until all I could do was dry heave. I didn't care; I wanted to please him.

"You like it when I choke you with my dick, don't you?"

I hummed in the affirmative. "Mmhm."

Bradley said, "It's good and wet now. Time to fuck your little ass.

The fear on my face must have shown because he sneered and said, "I said you were gonna like it, and I meant it. Don't give me that look. It pisses me off. Reminds me that I'm too big. I want you to pretend I'm just normal-sized, yeah?"

He took a tube of cold surgical lubricant and put a slippery finger in my ass. It went right in. It felt a little like rubbing a bruise but also familiar and safe. The pain of being fucked hard yesterday faded into the pleasure I'd felt with the big captain inside me. Bradley added another finger, then another. I pushed out like I was taking a shit, and something moved.

"You're dirty. Let's get you cleaned up."

He took me to the bathtub with one of those cheap plastic hand-held shower heads. He unscrewed the nozzle and set it on the counter. He ran the tub until the water was lukewarm, then said, "Come here!"

I stepped into the tub, not quite sure what he was doing. He put the open shower hose against my hole and flipped the bathtub off. The shower hose gurgled, then began pumping warm water up inside me.

"Tell me when it hurts."

"It hurts." He stopped the flow.

"Now hold it and go to the toilet."

I could barely keep the warm water inside me. I felt like a water balloon.

I sat down, and immediately a brown river flowed out of my loose asshole. When I looked, there were clumps of KY jelly, Vaseline, and old cum from Eric and Captain Harris mixed in with the poop. I flushed.

"You got a dirty pussy. Get back here."

I obeyed, and he reran it, this time ignoring my cries of pain. I pulled away, spraying a little water on Bradley before clamping down hard.

"You got dirty water on me. I'm not happy about it, either." He hauled off and smacked my face. It felt good.

I ran to the toilet again. This time, there were only a few moments where loose poop came out. The rest was a clear flow of water. Bradley checked before I flushed.

"One more time. This time, stay in the shower and shoot it at the wall. I want to see the whole thing."

He jammed the hose against my hole and filled me a third time.

"Okay, point it at the wall."

I sprayed a clear stream at the wall. I still felt full inside.

Bradley said, "Let's wait. There's always more."

Sure enough, I felt another wave of peristalsis, and I had to spray more water against the wall. It ran clear.

"You're ready. Let's go. When we do this again, I want you to be clean when I pick you up. You got that?"

"Aren't you flying out tomorrow?"

"Yeah, but I'll be back soon enough."

I felt giddy thinking about doing this with him again. I felt the warm tingles of puppy love until his lubed finger went in my ass, reminding me of the painful procedure I was about to undergo. He had three fingers in me when I squirted out another bit of clear water.

"You're lucky it was clean. You got more?"

I shook my head.

"Alright then. Help me with this." He gestured to his cock as he spread jelly up and down the shaft. I put both hands around it and spread the lube as evenly as possible. He put some more at the base, and together, we slicked him up good.

Bradley climbed into the bed and lay flat so his cock towered towards the ceiling. "Climb up on it."

I bowed my head obediently and climbed onto the bed, my feet straddling his hips. My short legs were just tall enough so that I could push the head up against my asshole. I tried to sit down, but only the small, pointed head went in. The corona was far too wide. I pulled up.

"Take your time, son. It's not gonna be easy, but I know you can do it."

I took a deep breath, then released it as I sat down again. This time, the little head pushed past my sphincter. It wasn't as little as it looked, sprouting from such a horribly thick shaft. As I pressed further, it felt like he was tearing me in two.

"Wait right there, kid. It's easier if you just wait."

I thought I would pass out; the pain was so bad. But he was right. As I waited, my ass loosened some more. I felt another inch go inside, then another, and then it stopped. He'd reached the end.

"Just ride it there for a while. We got time. I'm not gonna bust a nut until I'm all the way in past that inner pussy."

I bent and straightened my knees a couple dozen times, marveling at how far my ass had stretched. My little penis was drooling again. He was pressing that button so hard with his thick, wide cock. Each time I straightened my legs, the small head relieved the pressure. When I sat down again, the shaft squeezed so hard it felt like I would pop. It reached the back of my rectum.

Bradley shifted my weight. I felt the head push into my colon, then stop. I was sure he would tear a hole in me if he went any farther.

And he didn't go farther, not yet. He just lifted me gently up and down, letting the head slide in and out of that inner asshole.

"Kid, you got an amazing pussy. I'm gonna fuck you so good."

With that, he let me drop, catching me by surprise. I sat down hard before catching my legs and pulling up off of him. I felt like a sledgehammer had just pounded my inner pussy wide open.

"Quick, sit back down." He tugged me downwards, his little head entering my hole quickly, then sliding past the second hole. He pushed hard, and I felt several inches of shaft in my colon. The head poked against my little flat stomach. I lost my footing, and he caught me, lowering me inch by inch until I sat on his lap facing him.

He said, "I can see my cock inside your belly. You see that?"

"Yes, sir. I do."

He wrapped his arms around me and stood. I was impaled like a medieval Romanian soldier in front of Vlad's castle. I wondered if the cock would tear through me and come out of my mouth. I was glad he was carrying me because I felt faint and knew I couldn't stand.

He put a big hand on my small bottom and lifted me up, setting me back down hard. I watched the colossal cock snake its way through my colon. I felt his pubes tickle my bottom. Then he hit a spot I'd never imagined. I think it was the end of my sigmoid, where it meets the descending colon. It set off fireworks. I began to throb inside.

"Oh fuck, kid. Do you feel that? I do."

I wanted to nod, but I couldn't move my head. I was frozen in rapture. He set me on the cold desk, putting my ankles on his shoulders.

"Get ready, son. This may hurt, or it may not. Don't scream. Slap my arm if it's too much."

With that, he pulled back and forced his way in. I wanted to scream, but I wanted his dick even more. I bit my finger so hard it drew blood, but I kept it to a whimper. He didn't hold back. He fucked me over and over, bumping into my descending colon repeatedly, sending waves of peristalsis up and down my guts. I thrashed from side to side, unsure if it was pleasure or pain.

"See, I told you it was gonna be good. You like it, little faggot?"

I managed to say, "Yes, sir," before the room turned red. I might have passed out. The next thing I knew, he was holding my shoulders and fucking hard. The desk was just the right height, higher than the bed. He probably figured that out in rooms like this around the world. The desk, not the bed.

I looked at my belly, swelling and relaxing as he pushed in and drew back. The outline of his cock was as clear as it had been in his pants. I was tighter than a pant leg. I put a hand along the path where his cock protruded and rubbed my belly.

"Oh shit, kid. That feels so fucking good. Keep doing that."

With one hand, I stroked the expanding lump in my belly; with the other, I reached up and pinched his nipple.

"You're gonna make me cum if you keep doing that."

I twisted it.

"Shit, kid, I think it's too late now."

He sped up until his hips were a blur. My head lolled back onto the desk as I moaned quietly.

Without warning, my tiny penis grew rock hard, then spat a massive stream of jism on my belly and hand. Bradley saw it.

"Oh shit, I made you cum, no fucking hands. Oh fuck. Oh fuck. Fuuuuuck."

Deep in my belly, I heard a gurgling as my insides grew warm. His cum flowed through me, blasting my guts. He lifted me and carried me to the bed, where he collapsed on top of me, kissing me with his thick tongue. I kissed back, licking his teeth. He sealed our lips, and we shared breaths. He rolled over, still inside me. I felt him softening, but then my guts started to contract again. I couldn't help it. His softening reversed, and he grew hard again.

"Oh, kid, you want me so badly, don't you?"

"Yeah, I do."

"You want me to keep fucking you, huh?"

I nodded vigorously.

He rotated me on his hard cock, so I was face down. I felt my guts twist as he straightened out inside me.

"Bite the pillow; this is gonna be a while."

I felt his rhythmic humping, his huge dong sliding deep inside me. He took longer and longer strokes, pulling out beyond my inner pussy. When he pushed back in, it made a loud popping sound. The pops came quicker and quicker as he reached a breakneck speed. I surrendered completely, allowing my body's autonomic system to kick in. I shivered, twitched, and squeezed his cock with my guts. I had no way to stop it.

"You keep that up, and I'm gonna come pretty quick."

I said, "I'm not doing anything. It's my body."

Bradley fucked so fast that the gut popping sounded like applause. His hips smacked into my little flat butt cheeks, adding another sound to the thunderous clapping. My hips bucked without me.

"Your boy pussy is coming like a bitch, Willie."

"Unngh." I couldn't use words anymore. I was too far gone.

I bit down hard on the pillow. My penis was hard, dripping, and ready to shoot another load.

I whispered, "I'm coming, Daddy."

He put a hand under me and waited for me to shoot sperm into his cupped hand. I filled it up. He lifted it to my lips and made me drink before taking some for himself.

"Oh, fuck, that fresh cum is so good." He slurped and licked his hand.

He turned his attention back to my ass, fucking it hard and deep. I couldn't reach his chest, so I reached back and put my hands on his ass, pulling him towards me and releasing with each stroke.

"Yeah, spank my ass, boy."

I did my best with my skinny little arms stretched out behind me. I heard it make a little smack, barely audible over the thunderous pops in my colorectal junction.

"Do it again, but try harder."

I managed to smack him pretty good.

"Oh fuck, do that some more, I'm coming."

I was ready for it. I pounded Bradley's ass cheeks as hard as I could, punching them, slapping them, and pulling them close so he remained deep up inside me.

"Come inside me, Bradley. I want it."

"Shit, Willie, you know what I like to hear. Ohhh. Oh damn."

I felt his legs quiver, and he thrust forward so hard I hit the headboard. He stayed pressed inside me.

"Aargh! Oh fuck yeah. Take my load!" He

twitched and thrust, trying to go deeper, but he was already as deep as he could go. I felt the head touch that innermost magic spot, and then another warm, wet load cascaded from his pee hole, adding to the gurgling blockade of cum he'd already left inside me. I turned my head to look up at him. Beads of sweat trickled from his forehead, splashing on my cheek. I licked it, and it tasted like a grown man.

Bradley rolled, holding my belly, so we were spooning. In a minute, I heard him snore. His cock softened, but it was so thick and heavy I couldn't push it out. He held me in place, his cock lodged deep inside my little body. His hands rubbed my soft breasts as he slept. I heard him talk in his sleep, and then I fell asleep.

I woke to feel him pulling out of me. It felt like a boa constrictor was slithering through me, then I was empty. I gave a noiseless fart, and his cum pushed out onto the bed, leaving a big wet stain. It was mixed with a bit of blood.

Bradley said, "You should have waited. I was going to get a towel."

"I'm sorry, sir."

"No mind. It's nothing these maids haven't seen before. I'll call and have them make a fresh bed for me. I gotta get you home; it's nearly supper time, and I gotta fly to Tokyo in a few hours."

"When are you coming back?"

"In three days. I'll call you."

When I walked up the front steps to my house, I staggered. I didn't walk right for a week.

# 5

# ABANDONED

On the third day, I sat by the phone all day. It never rang. Maybe he meant that day four was his return. But he didn't call on the fourth or the fifth day. He didn't call at all. It was time to go back to school.

I didn't understand why he had kicked me to the curb. I was perfect for him, wasn't I? I loved his huge cock. He had to know that was worth something. Why did he just throw me away? Did he meet someone better in Tokyo? Was I no good in bed? I thought I'd been fucking fantastic. And still, he just threw me away.

I tried to hide my depression and tears from my parents, but they noticed.

"Willie, what's wrong?" My mother put a hand on her hip. "You know you can talk to us about anything."

I shook my head and chuckled. This was one of those situations that I could never, ever talk to her about.

"Mom, I'm just sad. Vacation is almost over, and I didn't get to hang out with my friends."

She smiled. "You were stuck to the phone all day, every day, just waiting for it to ring. I think you have a girlfriend you're not telling us about."

I thought fast. "She's not my girlfriend; she doesn't love me like I love her."

That didn't entirely keep them off my back. My mom kept telling me to call her. I would call POP-CORN, listen to the robot tell me the time, and then hang up. "No answer."

"Don't her parents have an answering machine?"

I shook my head. "Not yet."

On my flight back to school, they crammed me in economy class. It felt horrible after the intense pleasures of First Class. I sat next to a fat little kid who kept coughing on me. His mother did nothing to stop him. I cringed when they brought the food. It smelled like an unwiped asshole. I found myself crying into my chicken casserole. Bradley had left a massive hole in me, literally and figuratively.

The bitter winds blew over Boston as my taxi slipped on the icy roads towards my boarding school. I had friends there, but certainly not a lover. None of those boys were gay, as far as I knew, and I felt like the only fag in Boston.

※ 6 ※

# OUT OF THE BLUE

One weekend in February, I was watching Bewitched in the common room when a dorm mate poked his head in.

"Titty boy, you got a call."

I wasn't expecting a call from anyone. I worried it might be my parents with bad news. Grandma had been pretty sick during the holidays.

It wasn't my parents.

"Hey kid, whatcha doing?"

Anger and joy swept over me in alternating waves. I gave in to the joy.

"Bradley? I thought you forgot about me."

"My flight plan changed. I had to head to Australia, and it took forever to get back to Seattle. They had me in a Singapore/Sydney loop for a week."

"How did you find me after all this time?"

Bradley chuckled. "Well, I called practically every boarding school in Greater Boston, that's how. I couldn't remember the name of your school."

I was glad he couldn't see me blush.

"So I called around some more and finally found you. You wanna fuck again?"

"Yeah, but I'm on the pay phone. The guys can hear me," I whispered.

Bradley's breath grew heavy. "I really need to see you, kid. Can you go out?"

"Yeah, I gotta ask permission for an overnight."

"Do it. I'll pick you up in an hour."

I waited a few minutes in the icy wind until another rental Oldsmobile pulled up to the curb.

"Hop in."

On Route 2, sailing past the bare trees adorned with icicles, I asked, "Where are we going?"

Bradley put a hand on my thigh. "My friend in Waltham has a basement you're gonna like. He's having a little party, and you're the guest of honor."

My little pee-pee got hard imagining the type of party it might be. But it exceeded my imagination in every way.

❧ 7 ❧

# HIGH IN THE BASEMENT

We pulled up to the white house with aluminum siding and black window frames; Bradley leaned over and kissed my neck.

He said, "Okay, play it cool."

I smiled. "Sure thing, daddy."

Bradley kissed me deeply. My heart jumped. I thought it might be love.

When the door opened, I got an eyeful. Bradley's friend wore a leather jacket and pajama bottoms. I could make out the outline of a fat swinging dong that leaped to attention when he saw me.

"Bradley! I see you brought a friend to play. You must be Willie." He extended a hand. "I'm Greg."

I shyly shook Greg's hands, stealing glances at his growing cock.

"Take off your jacket and make yourself comfortable."

I looked around the room. I saw a blond cherubic guy in his twenties, a Hispanic man in his thirties, and a black dude in his forties. All told, there were five men, including Bradley. I was the youngest by half.

Greg said, "Gentlemen, shall we retire to the basement and show little Willie a good time? I hear he likes big ones like ours."

Bradley leaned over and whispered in my ear. "Me and these guys are like a club. We call ourselves the hangmen because we're all a little too hung for the ladies. I told them about your, uh, talents. They like little dicks, too. So you're quite the catch."

I blushed. I had a notion it would be a long, hard night.

Greg ushered me into the bathroom, where he'd rigged up a hose to his toilet.

"You know what this is for?"

I nodded.

"Good. Take care of it. I'll come to check."

He left me alone with the hose, which ran icy cold. I felt cramps as soon as the water filled my guts. After several icy blasts, I ran clear.

Greg came in. "Show me."

I inserted the nozzle, squeezed the trigger, and blasted my guts with the freezing water. When I stopped, Greg shook his head.

"No, keep going deeper." I was ready to burst, but I added more. It ran clear.

"Good. Now you're ready."

The basement was warm despite the bitter icy winds blowing just outside. Greg had a few space heaters to keep it cozy. It was almost like a sauna, in fact. I felt beads of sweat trickling down my neck.

Greg took the lead. "Get those clothes off. You'll feel better. Oh, how rude of me! I forgot to introduce you."

While I stripped, he introduced me. "This is Sven."

The blond guy gave a nod.

Greg continued. "And Pablo." The Latino guy smiled.

"Ey, what's up, man?" He had a Puerto Rican accent.

Greg pointed to the black man. "Herschel, this is Little Willie."

The guys were undressing. Sven took time to fold his shirt and his slacks. His jockey underwear bulged with promise.

Pablo was much quicker. He was already naked, his huge brown cock dancing halfway down his thigh. It grew as I looked at it.

Herschel was so black that he was purple. The head of his uncut cock throbbed and lifted off his leg. Greg's was the shortest, but it was still quite long, maybe seven inches, and even thicker than Brad's. He was going to hurt. They all were. I was out of practice. Sven's pink dick popped upward when he lowered his underwear, smacking his naked belly with a loud "thwack!"

What caught my attention after the cock show was a large metal contraption in the shape of an "X" in the center of the room. It had metal loopholes along the sides of the X. A thick easel pole held it upright.

Bradley said, "You like that, Willie? It's called a Saint Andrew's cross."

"Wh-what's it for?"

Greg produced four leather cuffs from a wooden chest on the table beside the cross. "Let me show you."

The fur-lined cuffs made my wrists feel pampered as he tightened them. He pulled on the leather straps until my hands were trapped.

Greg said, "Now step up. I'm gonna tie you."

I stepped up to the cross. "Do I turn around?"

Sven laughed and said, "We don't care much about your little dick, son, we want your ass."

I was pretty nervous about the whole affair. What if these guys were murderers? How would I get away?

Bradley sensed my hesitation and said, "Don't worry, kid, we won't do anything you don't like. Trust me; I know what you like!"

Bradley hadn't taken off his clothes yet. I guessed he didn't want to make the other guys feel inadequate.

"Don't be shy, son; step up to the cross." I obeyed.

Greg threaded the leather straps through the eyelets and tugged until I was spread eagle, facing the cross, my ass exposed. I was short enough that my stiff little penis just poked through the two lower legs of the cross. I was able to relax and hang limply from the eyelets if I wanted to. For the time being, I stood on the base of the cross and anticipated a good round of fucking. Bradley produced a pill and popped it in my mouth.

"Take a 714." He held a glass of water to my lips, and I obeyed.

Sven was the first. He slicked up my hole with mineral oil and spit, jerking his long, thin cock. It was definitely long enough to pass my inner pussy. I was excited. I hadn't been with a long, thin guy before.

To my surprise, Pablo stepped up and climbed the easel pole. I hadn't noticed the ladder rungs that sprouted from either side. His cock was level with my face. He had to bend to pull back far enough to get the head at my lips. I opened my mouth and took his fat head to the back of my throat. Sven cracked open a glass tube wrapped in netting and held it to my nose. The room spun, and my head throbbed. I scarcely noticed Sven's hard cock sliding up my shitter. I was out of practice, but it was like riding a bicycle.

Sven said, "Oh, yeah, this is perfect." He took a few shallow strokes. I concentrated on Pablo's long, fat cock, stretching my mouth.

Pablo said, "Yeah, boy, get it good and wet for me."

I did one better. I managed to open my throat, leaning forward enough to grasp hold of Pablo's butt, pulling him forward.

"Carajo! You are a talented little boy. Bradley trained you good."

I felt Sven pass that magic gate. My hole was so used to dealing with fat cocks, I just let him in. He held the glass tube up to my nostrils, and I swooned, letting Pablo deeper into my throat. I spied Herschel out of the corner of my eye, watching me getting impaled at both ends. He jacked his huge, greased-up purple cock. His skin gleamed in the bright lights of the basement. Then he stepped up beside Sven.

"Let me share him."

Sven stepped to my left, still deep inside me, and Herschel tugged at my right butt cheek, looking for a way in. This wasn't going to be easy. Sven gave me another whiff from the glass tube. I relaxed, and

Herschel took advantage of the moment. With a blinding burst of pain, I felt his fat head slip in beside Sven.

He said, "Oh, man, that's fuckin' cool."

Sven grunted. "It's tight now."

It was very tight. I wondered how I would keep from tearing in two. The two men were out of phase. I felt their cocks sliding in two separate rhythms, pushing past my inner pussy. Sven was slow and methodical. Herschel was fast and rough. He smelled manly and different. I liked the way he pressed against my side, thrusting violently.

Sven was silent, concentrating on depth and letting Herschel's fast-moving cock rub his. I heard a catch in Sven's breath that meant he was close.

Pablo made my throat throb.

"Pinche niño! You're gonna get me off." He pulled out, leaving me gasping for air. I saw his immense cock throb, strings of saliva stretching towards the floor. I thought he was about to paint my face, but he held his cock, waiting for the throbbing to go down.

Sven said, "Oh! Herschel, you're going too fast. I'm gonna—" and I felt a warm flood coat my insides. Cum leaked out in the spaces between his cock and Herschel's.

Herschel said, "Thanks for the extra lube."

Sven stepped away, his long cock snaking out of me and hitting his thigh with a gentle slap.

Pablo climbed down off the easel pole and came around. Now I had to be prepared for a truly painful double fuck.

"You ready? This is gonna hurt."

I nodded, excited to feel even more full than before. Pablo cracked another glass tube. It gave me a bit of a headache, but it did the job. Pablo slid up my cum-slicked highway, hitting the rear wall of my rectum. Catching a ride with Herschel, he pushed past my inner door into my colon and slid a little further and deeper.

When the heady chemical brew wore off, I whimpered. It really hurt. But I started to feel the effects of the pill come on. I was entering a soft, fuzzy place. The pain was intense but moving farther away. It was like the whisky on the plane but had no nasty aftertaste.

Herschel pounded me, grabbing my hair. "You like that, bitch?"

"Yeah."

He yanked my head, pulling my hair hard.

"That ain't how you respond to your masters, punk."

I said, "Sorry, sir."

"Okay then. That's better." His cock was huge but squishy, and it felt better than Pablo's, which was rock hard, stirring my guts like a paint stick. He was in rhythm with Herschel, sliding in on the outstroke; my boy pussy was getting hit twice as hard. And each time Pablo's rock-hard monster turned the corner, I came back into my body. The 714 was taking me away, but Pablo was bringing me back. I was grateful when he held the vial to my nostrils again. I inhaled deeply, thankful as the chemical took me away again. I looked down and saw a puddle on the floor below me. My tiny penis was drooling. Then Greg came around, kneeling, lapping up the sweet juice, and tickling my penis with his tongue.

He said, "Oh, your little clit is so tasty." The

words excited me, and without warning, I spat a load of cum, painting Greg's face. My loads had increased in volume since that first little spurt in the airplane bathroom. He stood, licking his lips and wiping the cum from his face, feeding it to me. I wanted him to eat it all. I was humiliated eating my own cum. My shame showed on my face.

Greg laughed. "You're gonna eat it, bitch." He smacked my cheek. I swallowed the rest.

Herschel's fucking was so fast that I lost my footing and hung from the cross, which only made it easier for him to fuck me as he held my waist.

Pablo groaned. "Oh, I'm gonna cum in this puto's ass."

Herschel said, "Shit, me, too." I imagined him grinning, but I couldn't see his face, no matter how hard I craned my neck.

Both men pushed forward hard and stopped. Their cocks throbbed, stretching my hole wider. Deep in my gut, they blasted my insides. It kept coming, filling my colon with jizm.

Herschel pulled out first, bringing both loads with him. Greg put a hand under me and caught as much as possible in his palm until it overflowed.

Pablo pulled out next, leaving my hole wide open. I couldn't close it if I wanted to. Air whistled out past my open anus, pushing more cum with it. Pablo caught it in his hand.

Then Greg fed me the first serving of the salty brew. It wasn't my own, and it tasted better. Pablo held up his hand, and I lapped it up like a kitten. I could almost taste Herschel's funky black essence mixed with Pablo's spicy Latin gravy. I knew then that I was a cum eater.

Before my hole could close, Greg stepped up and pressed his head against it. He was nearly as thick as Pablo and Herschel combined. I was fully warmed up, and with the pill kicking in, I felt him sail past my sphincter with the ease of sausage filling a casing. I was plenty stretched. His head knocked against the end of my rectum.

Greg said, "You like that, Willie?"

"Yes, sir."

"Good, because it takes me a long, long time. You'd better like it!"

"I love it, sir."

Greg hammered over and over, too long to fit completely, too fat to turn the corner. I felt pressure against my bladder. With each thrust, it intensified.

I saw Bradley out of the corner of my eye. He winked.

Greg turned to him and said, "Oh man, Brad. You outdid yourself with this little guy. He's a fucking little whore for dick."

Bradley chuckled. "It's amazing what shows up in First Class."

I said, "Sir, I have to pee."

Greg said, "Hold it!"

"But—"

Greg smacked me hard. "Don't talk back, you little cunt. Hold it."

I looked pleadingly at Bradley.

"Greg, the kid's gonna piss on your floor. You know what your cock does to guys. He's still new to all this."

Greg sighed. "Fine. Get that bucket over there."

I knew what would happen next but didn't dare say anything.

Greg was furious. "Don't hold back; piss in the fucking bucket!"

I tried, but my tiny penis waved about as the piss exited, spraying into the air in circles. I clenched, in dire pain so that I wouldn't piss anymore.

"Jesus fucking Christ, do I have to do everything?" Greg reached around and roughly grabbed my little nipple of a dick, pointing it at the bucket. I sighed and let loose.

Greg snarled. "You're so small, it's getting on my hands." He tried to stretch it more, which pinched my urethra, causing the piss to spray.

"Fuck!" He relaxed the pull and let me finish. He held his wet hand to my mouth. I knew what I had to do. I licked it clean. When I finished, he wiped his calloused hand on my back. The last few droplets came out as he punched my guts with his fat cock.

I lifted my hips, thinking that maybe I could get him to slide into the next chamber. To our mutual surprise, it worked. It didn't hurt much after the double fuck I got from Herschel and Pablo.

"Shit, kid, is that what I think it is?"

I nodded. Greg held me by the hair and roughly kissed my cheek. "You're a fucking miracle."

He grunted. I was relieved he had stopped hitting my bladder with that meat cudgel of a dick. His fat cock head punched through my inner pussy. It felt better, and then it felt amazing. My guts churned with those spasms I'd yearned for. My rectum squeezed and cramped against Greg's fat chunk of meat. I was coming like a girl again.

Greg's breath tickled my ear. "What is that?"

I said, "My girl orgasm."

Bradley said, "He comes like a girl when the dick is just right."

Greg said, "I never felt anything like it. Oh, man. It's so good. Did he do this with you guys?"

The three men who'd already violated me murmured "no's" and "nuh-uhs." I heard some bitterness in their voices.

"You don't know what you're missing."

Greg hadn't lied. He took a long time. I couldn't stop quaking inside, which must have sped things along, but it grew bothersome after ten minutes of continuous internal orgasm. I leaned into the high from the pills. I drifted up and away from my body, watching from above as Greg's fat pole slid into me. I could still feel all the pleasure of being filled up, but it lacked the passion I'd felt with Bradley in that motel room in Tacoma.

Greg's rhythm changed. His breaths grew shorter. It was time. He held my waist, pressing deep inside my guts until, at last, the head popped through that inner hole for the last time. I grew warm as he filled me with his gooey cum. His furry chest, matted with sweat, soaked my back. When he pulled out, I tried to double over. The sudden hollowness was too fast. But the restraints held me in place, and I could only spasm and jerk like a marionette.

Greg playfully smacked my bottom. "You won't hear your farts for a month."

His cum ran down my tiny balls and dripped onto the concrete floor of the basement.

"He's all yours." Greg stepped away.

I shivered when I felt Bradley's small head brush my gaping hole on its way in. My rectum was puffy and sore from the beating it had taken. But the touch of Bradley's cock against my sore insides was like a sovereign balm. I tingled with every inch. When he turned the corner and pushed in deeper, I moaned.

"Am I hurting you?"

I shook my head. "It feels so good."

Bradley shoved hard. "How about now?"

Did he want to hurt me? He couldn't. "No."

"Perfect." I'd given him carte blanche to throw caution to the wind and fuck me senseless. And he did.

As stretched as I was, I only felt pleasure now. There was a profound connection as Bradley's cock rubbed my swollen insides. He was a part of me now. We were one, linked from cock to hole. My anus was a wedding ring, and his cock was a giant finger. We were whole. I shivered again, and the waves began coursing through me, causing me to shake. The others watched on with envy as I bucked and thrashed, scarcely aware that I was screaming with joy. When he leaned forward and nibbled my earlobe, I lost it.

"Oh! Yes! Fuck! Fuck me! Fuck me hard!"

This time, Bradley obeyed my command. His hips thrust hard against my backside, and the hole inside me clapped like a standing ovation. I leaned my head against the cool steel of the St. Andrew's Cross, submitting entirely to Bradley's masterful fucking.

He whispered in my ear. "Kid, I'm starting to fall in love."

Those words alone caused me to ejaculate, adding to the mess on Greg's floor. I heard whistles and catcalls from the onlookers. We were putting on a show worthy of Broadway.

With each thrust, I said the words in succession. "I... love... you... I... love... you."

A static spark crackled between his pubic hair and my sweaty back. He bucked in surprise. "Oh, man!"

It was a magic spell casting its love over us. We joined together, and nobody could stop us. Not any more than I could stop the invasion of my guts. I was too loose to protest, so Bradley's cock swelled to its maximum girth, pushing aside the swollen lining of my innards and creating a slick highway for him to invade me. I was Normandy, and he was the United States. I waited eagerly for his troops to come ashore.

I gathered my strength and tightened my sphincter, caressing the girth of his cock.

"Keep doing that. It feels good."

I squeezed and released many times. "How's that?"

"Perfect."

I had relinquished my power. I was prone, immobile, spread-eagle on the metal X. I submitted to his cock, letting it rule me. It was the king of my insides. His precum made the highway more slippery. He gathered speed. I was entirely his. The pill had turned me into a rubbery, submissive mess. I didn't care that my boobs were jiggling. I didn't care that my penis was small. All I cared about was the cock moving through me and the bulging sensation that made me come like a woman. The slick, greasy pole in my hole. The fusion with another man, one who might just grow to love me like I loved him.

I couldn't control my mouth, either. "Oh, god! Oh, god! It feels so good!"

I heard Herschel say, "He didn't say that to me."

I giggled. I didn't say it because I didn't feel it. I was Bradley's boy now. He could loan me out, but I belonged to him.

"I'm yours."

Bradley said, "Yeah, I own you, bitch." It wasn't as mean as it sounded. He said it gently. I wanted to be owned, anyway. I didn't care if I was a bitch, a whore, a lover, or a piece of meat. I was his boy, and he was my big daddy.

As the room spun about me, I heard that catch in Bradley's breath. It's a universal signal that the train has left the station. My ears tingled with the air moving past.

"Come inside me!"

Bradley pulled out. "Not until I say so."

My hole throbbed, hungry for his cock. He waited a full minute, each second increasing my craving for him to return. He pushed back inside me slowly, letting me savor each inch as it crawled through my guts. I wriggled and squirted another load as he pushed past the second hole. The pleasure of his body pressed against mine was so intense that I barely noticed my ejaculation.

My head danced with visions. The pill caused them, but only in part. The sweet pain of his giant cock made me mad with lust. Again, his breath caught. This time, I didn't say anything. He would come when he said so, not me. I was his property, not his master. I was his willing slave.

Bradley's shallow breath tickled my ears once more. The hairs on my neck stood up. I wanted so badly to command him to come, but I knew he would torture me with a longer wait. I needed his sperm inside me, coating my guts. Then, he hit that spot where the sigmoid meets the descending colon; it made me lose control. I seized and squeezed, unable to stop the powerful waves traveling up and down my insides.

"Oh, kid, that's gonna make me--" He didn't have to say it because it started. I felt the warm bullet fire, filling me deeper than anyone else could. I yearned to wrap my arms around him, but I was tied to the cross. As if he could hear my thoughts, he enveloped my body in his strong arms, thrusting and coming. He yelled as he unloaded. I thought it would never stop. His embrace kept me warm, wet with his sweat. He kissed the top of my head and let me go. His cock still throbbed inside me, pushing out the last of his cum. We stayed locked together for a long time.

At last, he reluctantly withdrew, pulling his load behind him. As it poured out, he caught it and fed it to me. I somehow managed to hold my hole closed between handfuls so he wouldn't miss a drop.

When, at last, I had eaten it all, he said, "Alright, boys; who's ready for round two?"

# EPILOGUE

I got into Harvard with a scholarship that Spring. Bradley's home in Somerville was just three blocks from campus. He admitted that he'd picked up more than a few freshmen and brought them home over the years. Few stayed. Most left, frightened. I told my parents I had found an inexpensive apartment near campus, which would save them a ton of money.

Bradley came to my graduation and sat at the back. That summer, I moved into his place. When he was away on a flight, I pined for him. When he returned, he'd stuff me full of cock and cum until we collapsed, exhausted. On more than one night, we fell asleep, joined together, his cock deep inside me.

The semester started; I couldn't get my fill of Bradley's cock. There were days I dragged myself to class, dripping cum out of my gaping asshole. Nobody knew - I wore black jeans and thick underpants, switching to long johns and lined pants in Winter. Bradley still loaned me out on Saturdays to Greg and his rotating selection of friends. I never fooled myself that this was an equal relationship. I was Bradley's rental property, and he was the land-lord. He decided who got to live inside me. I took all tenants, sometimes a pair of roommates, in my cavernous hole. They never stayed long, just enough to fill me with their sperm and make way for the next renter.

As I grew older, my testosterone finally kicked in. I began to show a beard and pubic hair. My penis never grew, I was as tiny as ever. It no longer mattered. I liked a man with a big cock, and my little dick seemed to attract them like flies.

I was a popular guest at Greg's. The Hangmen, it turned out, was a rotating group of at least twenty top men. They came from all walks of life, but they had one thing in common: they were all very well-endowed. They showed up in Greg's dungeon whenever they could, so you never knew how wild the party might get. There were other men who offered up their holes to the Hangmen, too. But I was the most popular. Some nights, I serviced fifteen men; other nights, just a handful. Many wanted to own me, but I was Bradley's toy, not theirs. They could play with me, but they had to give me back in one piece at the end of the night.

Bradley was the biggest overall, but a few men were longer, or thicker. If they weren't thick enough, two was better than one. My ass hung like a pouty face at the end of a Saturday night party, but it was a tight smile by the next weekend. Except for those vacation weeks when Bradley took time out of his busy schedule to play with his beloved toy all week long.

# MILES HIGH

by Peter Schutes

# MILES HIGH

Jeffrey clutched his ticket in sweaty palms. He didn't like flying. Whenever he had a choice, he took a train or a bus. This was a transcontinental flight on a DC-10 from Los Angeles to New York. He could choose between three days of solid discomfort or six hours of terror...each way. But the meeting was tomorrow, so he had no choice.

Jeffrey ducked into the restroom for a quick pee before the boarding began. He groaned when he saw the urinal, a single trough. He hated other men looking at his depressingly tiny penis. He scanned the stalls to see if a private toilet was available; all were occupied. His short pause caused a gentleman to bump into him.

"Ey, are you going or not"?

Jeffrey turned to face his antagonist and almost wet himself on the spot. It was Ashe D'Estende, the straight porn star. The star saw the flash of recognition in Jeffrey's eyes and grinned.

Jeffrey turned red. He stepped forward to the trough and removed his tiny wiener. Ashe appeared beside him. He saw the small manhood and whistled.

"That sucks, man."

Jeffrey couldn't believe this blockhead. He also couldn't stop staring as the oaf peeled his skin-tight polyester pants from his thighs in order to extract his legendary dong. It flopped like a dead snake out of his trousers. It was so long that the head crash-landed in the river of urine below. Ashe cursed and lifted the monster out of the trough.

Jeffrey whistled.

"That sucks, man."

Ashe chuckled as the stream of urine trickling from his urethra became a rushing rapids. Jeffrey was so piss shy, he started to put it away.

"Where you going? Let's cross swords."

Ashe had an easy comfort with his body; it was contagious. Jeff relaxed and let the stream of urine flow from his little penis. Ashe swatted his stream of urine so it collided with Jeffrey's. Jeffrey swatted back, causing droplets to splatter the wall above the trough.

"Nice! You win."

"I win? That's a first."

Jeffrey's self-loathing colored his speech.

The loudspeaker announced the boarding of flight 1480 from Los Angeles to New York.

Both men put away their respective manhoods and left the restroom.

Jeffrey was not a virgin, but he had a hard time connecting with men. His small penis shame was a constant drum in his ears while he talked to guys. They sensed his fear and avoided him. It landed him on an analyst's couch for years.

Jeffrey gained most of his sexual gratification in erotic cinemas like the Pussycat on Western Avenue.

He would sit on an empty row and masturbate to adult movies. It was not sex, but it was easier than dealing with potential humiliation in the bedroom.

Jeffrey's surrogate sex life was the reason he recognized Ashe D'Estende. He was a French Canadian who came to Los Angeles seeking stardom, and his dick made him famous. It was, far and away, the biggest hard cock Jeffrey had ever seen. Soft, it was enormous. Rumors surrounding his legendary member were whispered in soft tones at the theaters. Several stars refused to work with him because he preferred anal. The women didn't have the guts to take the legend.

Thinking about Ashe took his mind off the upcoming flight. The gate agent took his ticket and sent him down the long, covered walkway to the jumbo jet. Jeffrey liked the covered walkway. The last time he had flown, he was forced to walk on a noisy tarmac as planes roared down the runway nearby. This quiet, climate-controlled hallway was a great improvement. When he stepped into the plane, he was astonished by its size. How could such a massive object ever get airborne? He had requested an aisle seat, hoping it would keep him from seeing the plane leave the ground. When he found his seat, it was occupied. By Ashe.

"Uh, I think this is my seat."

Ashe grinned. He took his ticket stub out and compared.

"Nope. Lucky, you got the window."

"Damn. Do you want to switch"?

"Hell yeah."

Ashe undid the seatbelt and adjusted his huge soft cock so he wouldn't sit on it when sliding across.

It snaked its way down his trouser leg towards his knee. While scooting, Ashe held the monstrosity with both hands to keep it from slipping under his thigh.

Jeffrey watched in envy and fascination. His mouth hung open. He felt faint. Seeing Ashe pissing was not even as interesting as watching him struggle with simple movement.

"Fucking huge, right"? Ashe grabbed a portion of his long meat and shook it for Jeffrey's benefit.

"Y-yes, sir." Jeffrey didn't know why he said that. Ashe made him want to submit.

Ashe's eyes sparkled. "Sir? Quel surprise." The Québécois revealed his origins with his accent.

Jeffrey sat beside him. He leaned forward to put his knapsack under the seat and caught Ashe staring at his ass.

Ashe sucked air through his teeth. "Bel cul, mon frere."

A rush of erotic pleasure surged through him. The biggest cock in porn was complimenting his ass.

The stewardess was demonstrating the seatbelt and the flotation device. Jeffrey looked at the placard studiously, prepared for the inevitable crash landing over water. Ashe watched as thin beads of sweat rolled down Jeffrey's face and splashed on the card.

"Eh, mon ami, are you frightened"?

Jeffrey nodded.

"I will help you. You must be distracted."

As the plane backed out of the gate, Ashe put his big meaty hand down the back of Jeffrey's pants and fingered his asshole. He leaned in and whispered, "Once we are in the sky, I will take you to heaven."

The plane gathered speed on the runway. Jeffrey

cried out as Ashe put one, then two fingers in his ass. The aircraft lifted off; Ashe slipped a third huge finger into Jeffrey's hole.

Ashe stretched and fingered him until the no-smoking sign turned off. By the time the stewardess walked past, Ashe was sniffing his fingers and smiling at his astonished seatmate.

"No smoking sign is off. Meet me in the back." He pulled a joint out of his shirt pocket and winked. He climbed over Jeffrey, making sure to rub his crotch in the man's face.

Jeffrey couldn't process everything that was happening to him. He was airborne, flying over some shitty suburb, and the hottest man in porn was waiting to get stoned with him. And he was too turned on to be scared.

Jeffrey undid his buckle and walked through the smoke cloud at the back of the plane until he reached the restrooms. All the stewardesses were busy preparing food at the front of the aircraft. Ashe stood just inside a restroom, beckoning him. He stepped in, and Ashe locked them in.

Ashe fired up the joint and passed it to Jeffrey.

Jeffrey coughed and laughed as they finished the joint together. Ashe flushed the toilet to change the air in the tiny room. He smiled at Jeffrey.

"You have a beautiful tiny penis."

Jeffrey reddened.

"No, no mon ami, it is a compliment."

"In what world is that a compliment"?

"I like to fuck handsome men, but only if they have itty bitty penises."

"I would have thought you preferred big guys, like the ones you work with."

"I am not a narcissist. My huge cock is beautiful, eh, but it needs not see its reflection, yes"?

His French Canadian accent was unattractive but sexy nonetheless.

"I don't understand."

"Let me show you." Ashe planted his lips on Jeffrey's and filled his mouth with a thick tongue. The passion, fueled by weed and high altitude, drove the men wild. Jeffrey tore at the pearl snaps of Ashe's cowboy shirt. Ashe removed the young man's trousers in one swift motion. He unzipped and extracted his rapidly growing member from his double-knit trousers. He applied airline lotion liberally to his cock and Jeffrey's asshole. The three fingers found their way in. Ashe had been fucking ass on camera for five years. He was an expert. Jeffrey moaned as his rectum loosened under the digital assault. He had never been with a masculine man. His dates were usually very feminine and always disappointed in Jeffrey's little unit. Ashe used his free hand to wiggle Jeffrey's scrotum and penis like it was a pussy. He felt like a woman; it was a huge relief. He didn't want to be a man with Ashe; he wanted to be a lady under his command. He knew he was about to be anally massacred, but he welcomed it.

The tiny restroom could not accommodate Ashe's manhood. He had to point it skyward to allow it to grow to its full length. Jeffrey felt the head slither up his back as it grew to its full length. He gasped when Ashe lifted him aloft as if he were a piece of carry-on luggage.

The lotion-slick head found its way easily into the finger-stretched hole. Ashe was tapered; his cock grew thicker towards the base. Jeffrey could handle the first few inches, but the last few were going to be murder. Ashe knew his body well, having stretched hundreds of asses on film. He nibbled on Jeffrey's earlobe to distract him from the blinding pain to come.

Jeffrey was confused. Ashe was supposedly straight, yet he wanted to fuck Jeffrey because he has a teeny weenie peenie. He wanted to spend more time analyzing the strange psychology, but his ass was screaming. Ashe was halfway in, and he'd already reached the end of the rectum. But then Ashe did something magic. He turned a corner and continued up Jeffrey's poop chute. It was blissful and intensely painful in equal measure. He whimpered.

"Sh-shh-shhh. Mon ami, you will soon feel only pleasure." Ashe caressed Jeffrey's small genitals. He rubbed the little head until clear juice dribbled from the tip. Ashe licked the nectar from his fingers. "Ohh, man, you taste sweeter than pussy."

Jeffrey could not hear the compliment. His anus was a flood of searing hot pain. Ashe was now two-thirds of the way into Jeffrey. His massive cock was moving deeper into the sigmoid colon.

Ashe was big around as a summer sausage near the tip, but he was thick as a wine bottle at the base. As he continued to lower Jeffrey onto his meat, the young man's rectum stretched beyond the limits of his imagination. He was careful to lift Jeffrey up at intervals to give his tight hole a chance to relax and recover. Then, he would lower him further than before. All the while, Ashe peppered him with kisses and whispered encouragement in his ear.

"Yes, you are doing it. You feel so good on my cock. You are a beautiful man."

Jeffrey winced and groaned. "You're going to split me in two."

"Relax, I am an expert. There will be no blood. Only deep satisfaction."

Jeffrey grew faint as the full realization of his conquest washed over him. Ashe had fully made a woman out of him. The gentle stroking on his genitals felt like he had grown a pussy, and Ashe was fingering him. Three-fourths of the way in, Ashe was forcing juice from Jeffrey's prostate.

The porn star cupped his meaty paw and caught the clear ejaculate. He sampled it, then held it to Jeffrey's mouth. He slurped his own pre-cum. It was delicious.

Ashe used the momentary distraction as a cover for his final thrust. He was balls-deep in his seat, mate.

Jeffrey's feet were back on the ground. He stood yoked ass-to-hip with the huge dick wedged fully inside his anal canal. He was invaded, conquered by this heterosexual porn star. He was a woman with a drippy clit.

"Are you ready for it"?

Jeffrey nodded, unsure what 'it' might be.

Ashe pulled back as far as he could and rammed his meat hard into Jeffrey's ass. He quickly withdrew as far as the tiny cabin allowed and pounded again faster. In seconds, he was fucking like a jackrabbit.

"Oh fuck! Oh god!"

Ashe smiled, "It's good, n'est-ce pas"?

"Oh, Jesus. Oh, Lord. It's...unhhh." Jeffrey lost his faculties of speech. He could only respond in moans, groans, and squeals of pleasure.

Ashe rutted his prey, dominating him, emptying

and filling him with his huge porn star dick. He loved nothing more than making a woman out of a man. He had wanted this man ever since he saw his small perfect cock at the urinal. He was straight on camera, but men with little dicks were his weakness.

Despite the confines of the cramped cabin, Ashe lifted Jeffrey and rotated him so his ass was on the counter, facing his anal invader. Jeffrey wrapped his legs around his intruder's waist. Ashe put Jeffrey's little cock in his mouth. He sucked and swallowed the pussy juice that oozed out with each violent thrust.

Jeffrey discovered Ashe's short circuit; he twisted his nipples.

"No, you will make me cum."

Jeffrey let his hands explore the round globes that formed Ashe's dimpled buttocks. They were lightly furry. Each thrust caused them to tighten. He put a finger between them, feeling the squeeze. He let the finger wander down to the puckered hole.

Ashe grabbed his wrist.

"The last thing that went in there was cut off. I am the man; you are my woman."

Jeffrey nodded. Ashe kissed him to ease the tension. "You may rub my butt, that feels good."

Jeffrey concentrated on Ashe's butt cheeks and powerful hamstrings, whose strength drove his massive member so hard into him. The unbearable pain had completely vanished. Each violent thrust of Ashe's elephantine dick brought only intense orgasmic trembling. Jeffrey's legs were shaking involuntarily. Ashe kissed his inner thighs and held his knees to calm him. Jeffrey saw stars. Pleasure washed over him in wave after wave. He had never felt this before. What was it?

"I made your ass have orgasms, eh"? Ashe wore a triumphant smile. "I can make it happen again and again."

He was right. Over the next five minutes, Jeffrey was reduced to a trembling heap of flesh. He melted into a warm buttery sea of anal orgasms. Ashe didn't stop. He lived to see that look of unrestrained ecstasy on his sex partner's face. Women were so easy. Only a few men could have multiple anal orgasms; Ashe had found one. He pounded and pounded until Jeffrey slipped into a trance. He lost control of his bladder, and piss poured out. Luckily, it ran into the sink.

"I fucked the piss out of you."

Jeffrey's head lolled. He looked like a junkie after a fix. The giant member in his anus was going to make him faint. The room turned red, and he blacked out. When he came to, Ashe was still fucking him deep and hard. He never wanted anything like he wanted this man's dick in him, but it was going to make him pass out again. In a gesture of self-preservation, he pinched Ashe's nipples.

"Are you ready for my cum, woman"?

Jeffrey nodded, focusing intensely on the porn star's leathery nipples.

"I am ready for yours, too." Ashe covered Jeffrey's tiny cock with his mouth and licked it like a clitoris. Jeffrey felt sperm building in his balls. The closer he got to cumming, the harder he twisted Ashe's nipples.

"Oh, fuck! You are making me cum! Ow!" Ashe

bucked and thrust, grinding his hips into Jeffrey's tight butt.

Ashe was first. Deep in the sigmoid colon, he let fly his first little spurt. Jeffrey felt it, and it sent him over the edge. He ejaculated his first squirt into the porn star's mouth. Ashe's second spurt was a flood. It felt like a sperm enema deep inside Jeffrey's bowels. Jeffrey, like Ashe, was a strong second shot. He was small, but he carried a huge load of cum. He squirted so much, so hard, sperm came out of Ashe's nose.

Ashe pulled back in astonishment just in time to catch a big wad of sperm in his eye. He opened his mouth and caught the successive squirts as best he could. Sperm got on his shirt, pants, and in his hair. Jeffrey was a lawn sprinkler.

Buried to the balls, Ashe kept shooting load after load up the small-dicked man's colon and anus. His legs buckled. Jeffrey's sperm half-blinded him. He looked like a glazed donut. Jeffrey stopped twisting his nipples. He leaned in and licked his own sperm off of Ashe's face.

Ashe grew soft. Peristalsis, so violently repressed by the gigantic anal assault, returned with a vengeance. Jeffrey ejected the porn star's huge flaccid member, releasing a torrent of baby batter in its wake. Ashe's gargantuan flaccid cock smacked hard onto the toilet lid on its way down. The rivulet of sperm puddled in Ashe's hand. He offered it to Jeffrey, who obediently lapped up the potent dick juice.

The two men breathed hard, looking into one another's eyes. Ashe took command, kissing Jeffrey as he lifted him off the counter. They cleaned one another with rough brown paper towels and warm airplane water.

"Wait a couple minutes."

Ashe opened the door, adjusted his crotch for maximum exposure, and walked past two stewardesses, winking. They both stared at his massive crotch; they didn't notice Jeffrey locking the bathroom behind him.

A few minutes later, Jeffrey limped back to his seat. Ashe gave him that winning smile and patted the spot beside him.

"Did I cure your fear of flying, mon ami"?

"That's putting it lightly."

He grimaced as he sat next to the best fuck of his life. Ashe offered him a cigarette.

"You will not walk normal for a few days. But it will feel good. You will remember me with every step."

"It hurts, but you're right; it feels great."

The two men smoked in silence. Ashe spoke.

"Do you want to do it again"?

"Hell, yes."

# CHOPPER JOCK

by Adam Maxwell Bigglesworth

# I

# RUDY

Rudy Acker flew the chopper for the local news channel. He loved his job, no matter how dangerous it might be. In the mornings, he flew with Gina Brightman, the traffic reporter. During the day, he sat around waiting for any police or highway patrol activity. He covered the evening commute and was on call for any late-night shenanigans between cops and criminals. It was an easy job and mainly consisted of traffic coverage.

Los Angeles was a vast city covering hundreds of square miles. Because Los Angeles traffic was a nightmare, a chopper was the fastest way to the scene of breaking news. Gina listened to the Highway Patrol radio to find the hot spots, and Rudy flew wherever she directed them.

Rudy loved his job, but he was lonely. Nobody at the news channel knew he was gay. He was afraid to come out. His secret was probably no big deal to the newsroom. Rudy was grappling with his demons.

The biggest demon was his dick. The damn thing was the average length, but it was thicker than a beercan. He'd tried to hook up with other guys. He didn't want to get fucked; he was strictly on top. The thought of sucking a dick or another man invading his ass was repulsive. He tried to dominate his tricks, but they all shied away. The guys would take one look at his huge fat dick and chicken out. If he was lucky, a few might agree to give him a hand job. The cocksuckers could cover the tip with their mouth, but nobody he'd ever met could suck him. He was basically a virgin.

Rudy had learned to hide his fat cock in loose pants. In high school, he wore Levi's 501 jeans to fit in, but the thick outline of his cock sent tongues wagging. He got too much attention from girls; the guys made fun of him. He was "Rudy Acker Tally-Whacker" in the gym showers. It didn't help that he had inherited an enormous ass, too. "Rudy Big Booty" still rang in his ears, even ten years after he graduated.

Rudy worked up his courage to go to gay bars. He wore the same tight 501s, hoping to attract a loose bottom, but everyone was a tourist. Not one greedy homo he brought home would so much as try it after they saw what he was packing. What was worse, his tight pants highlighted his round, firm ass, attracting other tops like flies. It sucked.

Gina Brightman was a friendly, funny reporter. She cracked jokes and kept Rudy in a good mood all morning. He worked nights with Mike Cole, who wasn't as interesting or funny. And when Rudy's evening shift was over, and he drove home to his apartment in Northeast LA, depression always set in.

Rudy kept a stash of glossy gay rags under his bed. It was Friday night, and he needed to get off.

*Boy Toy* always had the cutest young guys, so he picked up an old issue and flipped through, searching for a photo spread to assist him in his lonely ritual. He hit on a page he didn't remember. It gave him an instant stiffy - a piece called Bottomless Boy.

The subject was a slender young Asian man named Ho Lee and his encounters with two well-hung men. One man, named Richard DeCoque, had a very long cock of average thickness. The other man, Wolf Biggars, had a body just like Rudy's, including a furry chest and a beer can cock! The twink took each of them up his ass like a champ.

Rudy obsessed over the photo of the young man just after Wolf pulled out. His hole was a gaping cavern, dripping with cum. The look of satisfaction on the Asian man's face was a huge turn-on. Seeing a man who loved a thick cock like that made Rudy's cock throb.

Rudy took a few tissues out of the box and lay them beside him on his bed. He squirted a healthy gob of lotion into his hand and wrapped it around his meat. His fingers didn't touch.

In long, slow strokes, he went from the base of his cock up and over the corona. He made a ring with his thumb and middle finger and pushed down on his head until it snapped his fingers apart as he gripped tightly, returning to the nest of pubes at the root.

With his free hand, Rudy twisted a nipple. He was transfixed by the image of Ho Lee's gaping crack. Why had Rudy never found someone so talented? Would he have to hire a hustler? Could he hire Ho Lee? Rudy's nipples were wired to his cock, and it sent shockwaves of pleasure down the shaft to the spot between his balls and his asshole. His balls were alive, moving about like two kittens in a leather pouch.

He spoke aloud. "Oh, fuck yeah, I wanna fuck that hole. I'm gonna fuck that hole." The dirty talk pushed him along.

A thick tunnel, the corpus spongniosum, ran along the underside of Rudy's wide dick. As he pulled and stroked, it compressed, blocking some of the blood from leaving his engorged cock, making it thicker and longer. Having such a powerful image to jack off to was helping. He felt himself rocketing towards orgasm. He stopped, letting the impending ejaculation subside. Right at the edge.

When the throbbing slowed, he started up again. He fixated on the cavern between Ho Lee's butt cheeks. He had to look away, or he would cum. He closed his eyes, imagining the satisfaction of finally sticking his dick in a man's butt. He stopped tweaking his nipple to slow down the orgasm.

The lotion was drying out, so he took another big squirt. His hands and dick would be silky smooth before the night was through. He returned to the stroking, speeding up until he felt close and slowing down or stopping to let the orgasm abate. Rudy had stopped at the picture of the cavernous hole. Out of curiosity, he turned the page. The photoshoot hadn't ended like he thought. Ho Lee lay on top of Wolf, the incredibly fat cock stuffed back in his ass. Richard was squatting over the boy, sticking his cock into the same hole! The edges of the hole were an angry red. In the next shot, Richard pulled halfway out. The rectum stretched outward like a limpet about to latch onto the side of a fish. Next to the photo, it said, "Ho Lee has a pussy in his butt." The following picture showed both men buried to the hilt and the exact moment that cum flew from Ho Lee's cock. Puddles formed on his chest. He wasn't touching his cock.

That was too much. Rudy stopped stroking, but the orgasm had begun. He grabbed a hold of his cock, aiming for his chest, but he was too excited. A massive gob of cum hit him directly in the face. The next load was more powerful, landing in his hair.

He cried out. "Oh shit, oh motherfuck! Fuck! Yeah, I'm cumming in your ass!"

He closed his eyes and squeezed his cock with both palms, making a tight hole and pretending it was Ho Lee's ass. He shuddered as the last drops oozed from the tip.

The phone rang. It was the station. They needed Rudy for a police chase in Ontario.

"Shit!" He wiped up the cum and quickly hopped in the shower. His half-hard cock wouldn't go down because he couldn't shake the image of the handsome Asian man with the gaping hole taking two dicks at once. Rudy was prone to priapism, a long-lasting, stubborn erection.

The night reporter, Mike Cole, waited by the chopper. His eyes widened as he stared at Rudy's crotch. The persistent hardon wouldn't go down, and Rudy couldn't hide it.

"Damn, brother, that's a whopper!"

Mike wore a wedding ring. He had two kids. Rudy blushed, angry that his secret was out. Mike would tell two people, who would tell two people, and so on. His cover was blown. He cursed silently under his breath, then said, "Yeah. So what?"

Mike chuckled. "Sorry, man. It's huge. What do you want me to say? You must get all the ladies."

Rudy fumed. He flew the chopper in stony silence. They found the chase and followed the cops and crazed driver to Palm Springs, where the chase stopped on a desert road that dead-ended at Mount San Jacinto.

On the flight home, Mike said, "Hey, man, I'm sorry. Your dick is your business, and I was out of line."

Rudy sighed. "Would you do me a favor? Don't mention it to anyone."

Mike smiled. "If you let me see it, I promise not to tell anyone." He boldly placed a hand on Rudy's swollen crotch.

Rudy was a competent pilot. Surprised, he tilted momentarily, then brought the chopper upright. He didn't think married men cared about dick; he was wrong.

Mike squeezed. "Oh shit, that's fucking thick!"

Rudy nodded, unsure where this was going. He found out quickly. Mike unzipped Rudy's pants. He tried to get the monster out of Rudy's pants, but it was no use. He unbuckled Rudy's pants and unbuttoned them. It was trapped down the right leg. The impressive base, the thickest part of Rudy's cock, was exposed. Mike leaned over and licked the shaft. It felt good.

"Lift your ass, Rudy. I wanna see the whole thing."

Rudy thought about shutting Mike down, but then he thought, "Fuck it." He lifted his bottom so Mike could pull down the pants. The chopper reeled a bit as his hand struggled to stay steady on the stick.

The heavy cock broke free, lifting off Rudy's leg, begging for attention.

Mike licked his lips. "It's too big. I can't suck it."

Rudy said, "Then don't. Besides, I could lose my license."

Mike laughed. "Who's gonna know? They can't see us. We're five thousand feet in the air!"

For some reason, that turned Rudy on. Mike was right. They were untouchable. He didn't see the harm in letting Mike lick the tip. He'd never cum, but at least he wouldn't have to fight the guy off anymore.

Rudy said, "If you can't suck it, lick it."

Mike leaned over and ran his tongue up and down the shaft. He clamped his mouth over the head and swirled his tongue over the piss hole—the same boring shit.

Mike spat in his hand and stroked while he licked the tip. That was nothing new, but it did feel pretty good. Something about the altitude, the married man, and the thrill of doing something totally illegal excited Rudy more than usual. He felt his balls churn. Mike was a pretty good cocksucker. His lips stretched tight as he pushed as far as he could go without scraping his teeth or tearing his mouth open.

Rudy felt the man's tongue swirl around the head. He had never cum from a blow job, but this time felt different. He closed his eyes and pictured Ho Lee and his open anus dripping with Wolf and Richard's cum. He saw the two men's cocks stretching the hole. He thought about fucking someone like that.

"Mike, I think I'm gonna cum."

"Mmmhmm." Mike was in deep concentration, jacking and licking the massive cock.

Rudy was astonished when the first load came. It was his first orgasm by another man, and it was incredible. He let go of the stick, and the chopper dipped. Mike apparently didn't care. He kept sucking, unable to swallow it all, until the cum squirted out the sides of his mouth, staining Rudy's pants.

Rudy breathed hard as he took the stick and righted the chopper.

Mike wiped his grinning mouth, licking the remnants off his fingers. "Dude, that was fuckin' sweet."

Rudy smiled. It was by far the strangest and best sexual encounter he'd ever had. With a married man!

Mike said, "Do you ever fuck women with that thing?"

Rudy was puzzled. "Mike, I'm gay."

Mike shrugged. "I love pussy. But I can't stay away from big dicks. You're so fucking hot, you know that?" Mike put a hand on Rudy's chest and stuck his fingers between the buttons of his shirt, rubbing his chest.

Rudy was confused. He'd heard about bisexuals, but he'd never met one, and he didn't really believe they existed. He was gay, period. How could somebody be both?

Mike said, "I'd let you fuck me, but I can't handle that. I mean, I love 'em big, but that's ridiculous."

Rudy felt a surge of rage. "Okay, man! You think I like hearing that?"

Mike drew back his hand. "Oh, sorry. I mean, I'm pretty small. I thought big guys liked compliments."

Rudy said, "You think that's a compliment? I'm a virgin! I can't fuck anyone!"

Mike nodded. "Sorry. I didn't think about it. I've been with a lot of big guys, and they love it when I say shit like that. I guess the difference is I can take them. I'm sorry. I didn't realize."

Rudy's rage subsided. "It's just fucking frustrating. Nobody can take me. It sucks."

Mike said, "I wish we could share. I'd take a few inches from you."

Rudy sighed. "Yeah, that'd be cool. I'd like that. You got a magic wand? Do you know any fairy godmothers?"

Mike said, "I know plenty of fairies, but none of them are magic. I get sorta turned on thinking about it, though."

Rudy had to admit it turned him on, too. "Yeah, it'd be fucking great. I'd gladly give you some of this girth. It's too much."

They flew in silence the rest of the way to the heliport at Piper Tech.

When the chopper blades stopped, Mike leaned over and pecked Rudy on the cheek. "Your secret's safe with me, dude. Don't sweat it. And if you ever need another high-altitude blow, just say the word."

94

## ❋ 2 ❋

## DOUG

After that incident, Mike Cole sought every excuse to work with Rudy. As soon as they were airborne, his hand was down Rudy's pants, pulling the monster out to suck and play with it. Rudy started wearing sweatpants to make it easier for Mike to extract the heavy package. The flights were often too short, and Mike would have to start reporting. Occasionally, he would ignore the situation and suck on Rudy until he got a load of sperm out of him. This led to some stern reprimands from the producer, Tony. But Mike was dickmatized. He couldn't keep his hands off of Rudy's meat.

One night, there was a spectacular car crash during a police chase. Every other channel caught it, but not Mike. He was too busy slurping on Rudy's cock. When they got to the heliport, Tony Cazzone, the producer, was waiting, his thick, hairy arms folded across his broad chest. Rudy hardly ever saw him, so he knew it was going to be bad.

"What the fuck, Mike! How did you miss the car crash?"

Mike wiped Rudy's cum out of the corner of his mouth before answering. "What car crash?"

The producer turned to Rudy. "Where were you flying? Were you late?"

Mike stepped in, "No, sir. I missed it. Rudy had nothing to do with it. This is all on me."

As a consequence of his shitty reporting, Tony banished Mike to the newsroom for the foreseeable future. It meant that the sky-high blowjobs were over. Gina threw a fit when Tony tried to put her on the night shift, so they hired a new guy to start the following Monday. His name was Doug Chan, and he was a reporter from San Francisco; that's all Rudy knew.

The following Thursday, as Rudy was putting on his pajamas, he got a call from Tony, the producer.

"Rudy, there's a warehouse fire in the Toy District. We need you ASAP."

Thirty minutes later, Rudy pulled into the Tech Center parking lot. On the roof, the new reporter was waiting.

"Hi, you must be my pilot." Doug extended his hand.

"Hey, I'm Rudy." They shook.

"I'm Doug Chan." Rudy did a double take. Doug looked familiar.

"You fly this thing well?" The reporter waved a clipboard. The pen fell off. When he bent over to retrieve it, Rudy realized where he'd seen him. It was Ho Lee, the flexible porn star!

Rudy said, "Ho-ly shit."

Tony whirled around. "What did you say?"

Rudy bit his tongue and thought fast. "Oh, uh, I said, 'How did you like the job?'" He could feel the monster swelling in his pants. He was face-to-face with a porn star. And not just any star. This was a guy whose photos proved that he could handle Rudy's oversized cock.

Doug said, "This is my first chopper assignment. Let's go cover this fire, Rudy." His eyes darted downward, and he smiled. "Oh, what's this?"

Rudy turned beet red. He looked down, horrified that his pants were tenting outward. "I'm sorry."

Doug laughed. "Don't be. That's pretty impressive."

Rudy said, "Let's get to that fire. The clock is ticking."

Once they were airborne, Doug started chatting. "How long have you been flying?"

Rudy said, "Oh, eight or nine years now."

"Oh, good. I'm in good hands."

Rudy's head was reeling. He knew he couldn't say anything. The reporter had a past. It would be rude to bring it up. But each time he looked over at his passenger, his cock throbbed visibly in his pants. He couldn't get the image of Ho-Lee's— no— Doug's gaping asshole out of his head. His cock kept swelling. His baggy pants did nothing to hide his growing problem.

Doug said, "Are you always this excited? Are you a pyromaniac? Does fire turn you on?"

Rudy said, "Get your headset on and man the remote camera. We're almost to the scene."

An entire square block was roped off as a warehouse full of toys shot flames hundreds of feet in the air. The police and fire choppers took priority. Rudy and Doug had to work together to get a chunk of sky where they could get a good shot without interfering. They found it.

Rudy radioed the producer to make sure they were getting good tape.

Rudy said, "Hey, Tony. You getting this okay?"

Tony said, "Yeah. It's great! How's the new guy working out? Doug? Is he any good?"

Rudy said, "Yeah, he's on top of it. Like a pro."

Tony chuckled. "Interesting choice of words."

Rudy was puzzled but didn't think more of it.

It was a long night. The fire jumped to a second warehouse. Firefighters were injured. The news vans on the ground relayed information to the duo in the chopper so they could change angles and catch the action at the second warehouse. It was many hours before the smoke changed color, and the fire died down. Rudy could taste burnt teddy bears; his throat was sore. He looked at Doug, exhausted. "Good work, man. Ready to bring it home?"

"Yeah, let's go."

Rudy's chubby cock had subsided at some point during the night. The sun was just cresting the horizon as they brought the chopper down. He looked at the dawn light on Doug's handsome face, remembering the photo where he looked content with two cocks stuffing his hole. And crap! He was getting hard again.

Doug did a double-take. "Rudy, did you take Spanish fly? What gives?"

Rudy shrugged. "I don't want to get into it."

"Try me."

With a sigh, he said, "Doug, I'm gay. I own a lot of porno mags. So..."

Doug frowned. "You—you've seen me? That was

one time, years ago. Oh shit, please don't say anything."

Rudy said, "I was impressed. You're a pro."

Doug slapped him. "Do you know how fucking rude that is?"

Rudy recoiled, holding his cheek. "No, I'm sorry, I don't know. I've never met a porno star."

Doug turned crimson. "I'm a reporter. Got it? I did one photo shoot, and that's it. If you tell anyone, it will destroy me."

"Don't worry. I won't say shit."

They sat in silence on the helipad as the rotors came to a stop. The slap had tamed Rudy's hard cock. It was soft.

Doug said, "How about you? You must have done porn with a gate crasher like that."

Rudy shook his head. "I'm not good-looking enough."

"Are you kidding? Okay, A: you have that dick. I haven't seen it all, but it's massive. Huge. B: you're a handsome stud! That mustache, your big chest, you're the complete package. Believe me, you would make a fortune."

Rudy blushed. "You're pulling my leg."

Doug gave an evil grin. "Which one? You got three."

Rudy laughed. He took a risk. "You know I fantasized about you for weeks."

Doug said, "Weeks? So you don't fantasize about me anymore? It's been five years."

"I just saw it for the first time a few weeks ago."

Doug grabbed his clipboard. "I have an appointment with my mattress. Thank you for keeping me in the center of the action. You're a good pilot." He patted Rudy's leg and got down from the chopper.

"Wait!" Rudy hopped down. "Do you want breakfast? My treat." He was rarely this bold.

Doug's smile faded.

Rudy quickly added. "I mean, no big deal. I'm tired, too."

To their surprise, Tony, the producer, appeared. Rudy noticed a familiarity between him and Doug that he couldn't place.

"Hey, guys, great work. Rudy, I need you for the afternoon commute. We have Gina in the van for the morning commute. Go home. Doug, get some rest. 2 pm call time."

Doug turned to Rudy. "Rain check. Definitely." His pen fell from the clipboard. When he bent to pick it up, Rudy wondered if he'd done it on purpose.

# ❈ 3 ❈

# DETOUR

Rudy drove home to his little two-bedroom house in Lincoln Heights. It was a dodgy neighborhood, but he was nestled between two bare hills with a view of downtown in one direction and wilderness in the other. His bedroom was quiet. He could hear the occasional gunshots in the distance, but for Los Angeles, it was peaceful. The best part was the commute: a short drive down Alameda to the Piper Tech Center Heliport.

He tried not to think about Doug's ass. It was like trying not to think about a giraffe. It dominated his consciousness, making him hard again. He was too tired to jack off. After a restless hour or two, he finally drifted off to sleep.

When he woke, Doug's words resonated in his head. "You're handsome...you are the complete package...you could make a fortune." Why had it never occurred to him? Why comb through bars and bathhouses in search of the perfect bottom? Why not let a casting director do the matchmaking?

The phone rang. It was Tony. "Doug, we have a

situation on the 405 in Van Nuys. How soon can you make it?"

In 30 minutes, he was airborne with Gina by his side. They flew Northwest to the intersection of Sherman Way and the 405, where a ten-car pileup with an eighteen-wheeler blocked three lanes of the northbound commute. Their assignment was simple. Gina prattled on about the situation, passing along any updates she heard from the highway patrol. Nothing was going to change, so they didn't really need a lot of live footage. The newsroom could just clip any segment they wished from the hour-long shot of traffic at a near standstill. The next video they needed would show those magic moments when a lane opened, then another, and finally, the traffic would begin to crawl. But those moments were a couple of hours away.

With nothing to report, Gina made conversation.

"How's the new guy, Doug?"

Rudy thought carefully before answering. It was a trick question with no correct answer. "He's okay," he said.

"Okay, good, or okay, bad?"

Rudy shrugged. "He's fine. He's no Gina Bright-man. I'll bet you're relieved he took the night shift."

Gina snapped. "He's a job threat! I don't feel any relief!"

Rudy eyed her warily. "I just thought you'd be glad you got what you asked for."

Gina gave an apologetic grin. "I know. I'm sorry. It's just so hard to be a woman in this business. We have to work twice as hard to get half as much. No offense to men. Even a man like you has it easier."

Rudy's breath caught. What kind of man did she think he was?

"A man like me? What do you mean?"

Gina rolled her eyes. "Oh, come off it, Rude. I know why you don't have a wedding ring, if you catch my drift."

Gina had just ripped the covers off him, exposing him to a cold, harsh reality. "I, I, what are you talking about?"

She laughed. Not a vicious laugh. "Rudy, I'm a reporter. It's my job to gather facts. You and I both know what kind of man you are. And it's great! I love having gay friends."

Rudy was about to shout, "I'm NOT gay!" Then he realized it was too late. He had no reason to argue with his friend and coworker.

"Who have you told?"

She tilted her head. "Uh, no one. Why would I?"

Rudy eyed her warily. "I mean, does everyone know?"

Gina shrugged. "It's never come up. I doubt anyone knows besides me and Tony."

His boss knew? Why hadn't he fired him? "Tony?"

Gina said, "This is Hollywood, baby. Nobody gives a shit who you fuck."

"I never told Tony."

Gina punched Rudy in the arm. "Tony's gay. Can't you tell? Oh! And that new guy, Doug, he's a queen, too."

Rudy held the chopper steady with each new blow of information, threatening to take them into a nosedive. He wanted to land in the Sepulveda wetlands and crawl under a bush. When did it become okay to be gay?

Gina said, "Look, sweetie. You're an adorable gay man. You've got nothing to be ashamed of. You're not a reporter, so you don't have to worry about a scandal. Nobody knows you're up here with me. They just assume I'm flying the damn helicopter!"

Rudy had planned never to come out at work. He felt a rush of emotions—shame, sadness, joy, relief, and fear. He thought he might faint, which would have been deadly. He concentrated on the stick and kept the chopper steady as the unbearable flood washed over him. He didn't recognize this new feeling in its wake. He felt twenty pounds lighter.

Gina studied the pilot. "Oh, honey, you were hiding your light. You're a good man. I hope you know that."

Rudy wiped his eyes with the back of his sleeve. "Thank you, Gina."

Tony's voice crackled over the radio. "Guys, we got a situation in Simi Valley. A train derailed. Gina, are you ready to do some overtime?"

Gina said, "It's my husband's birthday. I can't do it. Send that new guy, Doug."

Tony said, "Come on, Gina. You're just a few miles. Tick tock!"

"No. Doesn't Doug live in Van Nuys? He can meet us at the airport."

Tony sighed. "Okay. Hang on." After a minute, Tony came back on. "He'll be there in ten. Gina, you're going to pay for the cab."

"No fucking way."

Tony said, "It was worth a try."

# FRENCH DIP

Rudy's heart skipped a beat when he saw Doug waiting by the helipad. Gina got out of the chopper, holding her hair to keep the beating blades from destroying her coiffure. She nodded at Doug and rushed toward the passenger terminal.

"Hey." Doug slipped into the reporter's seat. "Long time, no see."

Rudy nodded. "Nice to see you again, old friend."

The train derailment was pretty mild. Two cars were off the track, leaning to one side. Displaced passengers boarded buses bound for Union Station. Doug reported on the few injuries and got some excellent footage of paramedics loading a passenger onto an ambulance.

Tony sent them back to the 405, which was still blocked but due to clear soon.

The flight from Simi Valley to Van Nuys was five minutes. Doug broke the silence.

"I don't date at work."

Rudy said, "I didn't ask you on a date. I asked you to breakfast."

Doug said, "Okay, just dinner. How about after this? Denny's?"

"Philippe's," Rudy said, "I like the lamb dip."

Philippe the Original was and still is a busy lunch counter with great prices and good food. The famous story is that a server dropped a guy's bread in the juice from one of the roasts. He told her to leave it, and the next time he came, he asked her to dip the bread in the juice. The other patrons saw it and asked to try it. It became a sensation, and the "French Dip" sandwich was born. It was not a French delicacy but so-named because Philippe, the owner, was of French descent.

Rudy sat across from Doug, drawing spirals in the sawdust on the floor. He said it wasn't a date, but it sure felt like one.

Doug broke the silence. "I meant what I said. You're handsome and hung. You could earn a lot doing porn."

They used soft voices.

Rudy was intrigued. "How does a guy even get started with that?"

Doug said, "You get a referral from someone in the business. I've been out of the game a long time, but I still know a guy at York-Hawk Studios in Chatsworth. They'd hire you in a hot second. Here." He scribbled an 818 number on the napkin. Rudy folded it absent-mindedly and stuffed it in his jacket pocket, then said, "Would I have to fuck women?"

Doug laughed. "No, this is strictly gay. Do you have a lot of experience fucking men?"

Rudy felt comfortable with Doug. "I'm too big. I haven't found anyone yet. I'm still a virgin."

Doug's eyebrows went up very slightly. "It's that big?"

Rudy nodded.

"And you've never done it with another guy?"

Rudy shrugged. "I found someone who could get me off by sucking on the tip."

Doug leaned forward, whispering. "I can show you a thing or two if you are okay with no-strings sex."

Rudy felt his flesh swell in his pant leg. They were at a booth, but he knew it was so big a nosy passerby might see it. They were done with their sandwiches. Getting up was going to be horribly embarrassing. He flushed.

Doug said, "Did I say the wrong thing?"

Rudy shook his head. "You gave me a boner. I can't stand up."

"Put all your stuff on my tray and use yours to cover it." Doug ducked his head under the table. "Holy shit! Okay, there's a garbage can right by the exit where you can leave it."

Rudy should have thought of that. He put his coffee cup, paper plate, and napkins on Doug's tray, carefully covering himself as he stood up, trying to look casual. At the door, he put the tray on the rack above the garbage and pushed through the door. His car was back in the garage. He would have to walk a block and a half to the Tech Center with a raging hard-on. Doug had a wiggle to his walk that made things even worse. As they passed Olvera Street, a Mexican man saw it and jumped. "Ay, Dios!"

Doug saw Rudy's dismay. "Dude, you gotta own that. What you did to that guy just now, that's power. Take it. Use it."

Doug's words helped. The woman who clutched her purse and gasped made them both laugh. Rudy felt better about his ridiculously thick cock. He knew he was going to feel even better when he had jammed it into Doug's willing backside. That thought made his cock swell even bigger. The security guard at the parking lot exit saw it and whistled. Rudy waved back. It did feel powerful.

Doug didn't hold back when they got to his car. "You've got an incredible dick. That thing is huge!"

Rudy smiled. "You've got an unbelievable ass. I've seen what you can do."

Doug said, "It's all smoke and mirrors. It took more than half the day to warm up enough to take Wolf, and we had to go into overtime for me to take the two of them."

The drive to Rudy's little cottage on Alta Street took less than five minutes. Doug threw his coat on the couch and kissed Rudy hard. He put a hand on the salami-sized bulge and rubbed it. Rudy put his hands on Doug's ass, feeling the soft globes of flesh yield to his fingers. He licked his finger and stuck it down Doug's pants, exploring his hole. It was tight.

Doug said, "You'll have to use more than one finger to get me ready. Do you have lube?"

Rudy pointed to the Intensive Care lotion.

Doug sighed. "That's going to burn. I'll be right back."

Rudy rummaged through Doug's kitchen and returned with a can of Crisco. "This is perfect. Do you fist fuck?"

Rudy frowned. "No."

"What do you use it for?"

"Making pie crust and frying chicken."

Doug doubled over with laughter. "That's so cute. You are an adorable man."

It wasn't mean laughter, and Rudy joined in. He had no idea that Crisco was for anything besides cooking.

Doug took charge like a bossy bottom. He laid a towel on the bed and undressed. "Rudy, your hand's going to be greasy. Take your clothes off now."

Rudy liked the way Doug took a teaching role in the encounter. He was inexperienced. He'd seen guys fisting, but he'd never once tried it.

When Doug's underwear came down, Rudy was surprised by how long his cock was. It was above average, nearly as long as Rudy's. It was thinner than most, like a Persian cucumber. Doug was definitely turned on; his cock stood at attention. He got on all fours on top of the towel and wiped a small glob of Crisco on his hole, using a finger to coat the inside.

Rudy didn't know how much Crisco to use. He took a small amount and pushed it into Doug's ass, running his knuckles over the hole until his hand was shiny with grease. He started to push the whole fist in.

"Ow! Wait!" Doug grabbed his wrist. "Start with one finger and work your way up. I'm out of practice. My boyfriend is a lot smaller than you."

Rudy slipped in two fingers and felt the warm flesh engulf them. Doug breathed out hard. "Okay, now twist them so you can spread my hole apart a little."

Rudy opened his fingers like pliers, gradually stretching Doug's hole. He snuck in a third finger and made a triangle.

"Yeah, that's it, baby!" Doug pressed into Rudy's

fingers. As he pulled away, he let out a long sigh. "Okay, it's like riding a bike. I'm ready for your pinky."

Rudy slid in the fourth finger, rotating his hand to pull apart the ass lips.

"Oh, shit, that feels good," Doug said.

Rudy sped up, punching his four fingers into Doug. He tried to get the thumb in, but Doug held his wrist. "Not yet. Keep doing that."

It took another ten minutes before Doug let Rudy add the thumb, and he needed another twenty before he was ready for the whole fist. Rudy was impatient, and with his thumb touching his pinky, he pushed in all the way. Doug screamed.

"Oh fuck! Goddamn you!"

Rudy withdrew his hand, causing Doug to scream again. The neighbors were going to hear. It was a bit unsettling.

Doug bowed his head and hissed, "What are you waiting for? Do it again!"

Rudy obliged, popping past the sphincter. Doug jumped and wailed, but it wasn't a scream. Rudy knew what to do. He just kept pushing in and pulling out. Each time, Doug's protests were quieter until he was purring.

"Okay, now make a fist and punch it."

Rudy made a boxer's fist and pressed until it popped in. Doug shrieked. "Yes! Yes! Just like that! Oh fuck, just like that!"

When he pulled out, Doug's hole yawned, and a muffled roar of air came out.

"Okay, I'm ready."

Rudy used his fisting hand to spread a thin veneer of Crisco on his dick. Doug looked over his shoulder. "No, man, it's gotta be a lot more than that."

Rudy took a big scoop of Crisco and coated his cock until it looked like a frosted cake.

"Once your head is in, stop there. I'll need to adjust." Rudy looked down and noticed the head of his cock was indeed bigger than his fist. The shaft was thicker than his wrist, too. No wonder guys ran away screaming.

Rudy pressed against the hole, feeling it give way and then stop before he was in.

"Hold it there. Right there, like that." Doug cursed under his breath. "Shit! It's so fucking big."

Seeing his cock against Doug's big ass, Rudy realized he was probably a lot thicker than that porn star Wolf. He stayed still, letting Doug adjust to the first half of his head. He was throbbing with excitement, anticipating the first real fuck of his life.

"Okay, some more." As soon as Rudy pushed another fraction of his cock in, Doug put a hand on his thigh and pushed him back. "I don't know if I can take it."

Rudy thought he might cry. Then Doug said, "Just fucking push hard, I'll manage."

Rudy leaned into Doug, hearing his moans and cries as the head slid slowly past the tight muscle. Doug pounded the bed, howling. "Don't! Stop! Don't! Stop! Don't stop!"

Rudy kept pushing; then, suddenly, he felt an unfamiliar rush as Doug's hole sucked him in. His head was past the opening. Doug punched and bit the pillow. "Wait right there for a sec."

Rudy obeyed. Doug urged him on. "Okay, slowly. Your dick is thicker in the middle." Rudy held

Doug's waist and walked forward, feeling resistance as the thickest part of his dick passed the opening. Then there was that suction again, as the sphincter tightened, pushing his cock forward. He was all the way in.

Doug sniffled, wiping tears from the corners of his eyes. "Stay like that a sec. I gotta adjust." A minute ticked by. "Okay, go to town."

Rudy's hips knew instinctively what to do. With careful precision, he dragged the head to the hole's edge, then pushed it back to the end. As he hit the back of the rectum, it gave, letting him go right up to the bush.

"You can go faster." Doug wriggled, head down, ass up, looking over his shoulder at Rudy.

Rudy's hips gradually sped up like a train pulling out of the station. Each time he hit the back of the rectum, Doug gave out a little cry. His cock was soft now and looked very small, hanging between his meaty thighs. Rudy found his rhythm, about one second per stroke. He kept at it, feeling the gurgling in his balls that meant he was going in the right direction.

To his surprise, Doug's little dick started to leak. It wasn't precum. It was piss!

"Dude, you're fucking the piss out of me!"

Rudy paused. "Do you want me to stop?"

"No! Keep fucking me! It feels so fucking good."

Rudy watched as Doug soaked the towel with an intermittent stream of urine that peaked each time he hit the back wall of the rectum. It excited him. When all the piss was gone, Doug's dick stretched into a hard-on, throbbing in the air.

Rudy wondered how a man could let another man

fuck him. It sounded horrible. All that pain? Pissing himself? It had to be humiliating. But he put his mind back on the task at hand.

Rudy was so used to jacking off that it was taking a while. His hand could move much faster than his hips, or so he thought.

Doug said, "Faster! Harder!"

Rudy sped up until his hips were a blur, smacking hard into Doug's backside. The sight of his cock disappearing into that hole pushed him closer.

Rudy went so fast that his cock started to pop out. He saw the gaping hole, willingly sucking his cock back inside, and it was the tipping point.

"Oh, shit, Doug, I'm gonna come."

Doug's face was buried in the pillow. He moaned, but no words came out. Then Doug's long, thin cock shot a massive, hands-free load onto the towel. That was all Rudy needed.

"Here it comes!" Rudy felt his balls churn, and a hot stream of cum raced up his shaft. It blasted into Doug's completely stuffed hole. With nowhere to go, the cum blasted out of Doug's ass and coated Rudy's legs and pubes. It kept coming, running onto the towel. Rudy stayed buried until the throbbing subsided. His cock softened, and Doug's rectal muscles forced him out. The gaping hole released a dribble of cum that ran down Doug's balls and onto the towel.

Doug stayed face down, buried in the pillow. When Rudy shook him by the shoulder, he rolled onto his back with a wide grin.

"Fuck, Rudy, that was incredible. I won't feel my boyfriend's dick for a week."

Rudy felt powerful hearing Doug's compliment. A porn star told him he was incredible!

"Can we do it again?" Rudy wanted it to be a regular thing.

Doug said, "I told you no strings attached. Remember?"

"But I thought it was incredible!"

Doug sighed. "I'm in a relationship. I can't fuck around like this. As it is, he'll probably notice when I come limping home. God, I can still feel the wind in my ass." He dressed quickly. "Can you take me to my car?"

# 5

# THE CLUBHOUSE

The drive back to the parking lot was awkward for both men. Rudy felt hurt that Doug pushed him away. At the parking lot, Rudy said, "Doug, where am I gonna find someone else like you? You're all I've got."

Doug said, "Call York-Hawk Studios. They'll hook you up. And if that doesn't work, there must be a half dozen fisting clubs in LA. Just go to one of those."

Rudy's ears perked up. "Where do I find them?"

Doug rolled his eyes. "Go to a newsstand and get the Advocate. There's classifieds in the back. You'll find them."

"I had a great time!"

Doug was cold. "Yeah, whatever. Next time, I'm fucking you, though."

The words "next time" lifted Doug's heart with a smile, followed quickly by the awful notion of getting fucked. He couldn't hide the horror on his face.

Doug said, "Hey, turnabout is fair play. If you ever want to fuck my ass again, you gotta try it first."

"Well," Rudy thought, "That's not gonna happen." He drove home with mixed feelings. He'd lost his virginity, a reason to celebrate. Doug was a great teacher, but he went too far when he brought up the idea of him fucking Rudy. It made him sick to his stomach. He didn't want that. His ass was for pooping, nothing else. In the dark recesses of his mind, he was curious why so many guys liked it. It had to hurt like hell. But maybe, just maybe, he was missing out.

On his way home, he stopped at a newsstand in Chinatown. He found the Advocate. When he got home, he was astonished at the variety of ads and articles. He had been too isolated as a gay. Doug had acted as a tour guide and a teacher, showing him the answers to his problems after so many years of isolation and virginity.

He found a fisting club in Silverlake called the Clubhouse that met on Sunday afternoons. He always got lost in Silverlake. Too many streets turned back on themselves because of the hills. Streets that ran parallel crossed at right angles. He got out his Thomas Guide to figure out the location and wrote down turn-by-turn instructions to get there.

His stomach jumped with butterflies as he drove to the address on Hyperion. The Clubhouse was a dark storefront, something you might walk past a dozen times and never notice. The ad said it started at 3 pm, and he was too early. He saw someone knock, and the door opened, admitting them. He knocked.

A strange old man with glasses, a cane, and a white beard answered. He looked Rudy up and down, lowering his glasses to examine his bulge.

"Oh my. You've certainly come to the right place,

son." The old geezer reached out and gave an impolite squeeze. "Damn!"

Rudy hoped the other club members were less of a turn-off. The guy saw Rudy's dismay. "Don't worry. I'm the old geezer who runs the place. Name's Clovis."

"I'm Rudy."

Clovis said, "We get plenty of young folks here. You're early, though. Shall I give you a tour?"

Rudy was astonished by the bold layout of the place. A dozen leather hammocks (called 'slings,' he later learned) hung from the rafters. Each hammock had a stool in front, and on each stool was a can of Crisco.

"We got hobby horses in the back if you prefer that. I assume you're a top?"

Rudy nodded. He said, "I, uh, I've never been to this kind of place before. Sorry."

Clovis gripped Rudy's arm. "Oh, my. A novice. Shall I explain how it works?"

Rudy said, "Yeah, I think so."

Clovis set about describing how the club worked. He said that bottoms climb in the slings once the bell rings, and tops choose their partners in a round-robin fashion. The half dozen hobby horses were padded benches for men to lean over and take whatever the other guy was giving. "Needless to say, there are way more bottoms than tops; it's Los Angeles, after all. A top like you, you'll have your pick of the litter. Here, have a beer on me."

Clovis cracked open a Coors for Rudy. The cold brew settled his nerves. He watched the door as an assortment of men came through. There were middle-aged dads, high school dropouts, bodybuilders, hairless pretty boys...the whole spectrum of Ange-lenos. As they drifted in, they ordered beers and sized each other up. A few guys whispered and pointed at Rudy. It would have pissed him off, but he was learning to enjoy the attention of men, even if most of them were too cowardly when faced with the monster.

A thin, delicate man with frosted hair and a shiny, new-wave suit approached Rudy and said, "Ooh, look what she's packing!" He placed a dainty hand over the massive lump and squeezed.

Rudy sized up the thin-waisted queen. "My dick is wider than your hips. There's no way you can handle all this." He pushed the hand away.

"I like a confident top. I can't wait to prove you wrong. You do know what kind of club this is, don't you?"

Rudy snorted. "Trust me, sister, you won't be able to handle it."

"The name is Tosh, and I would wager twenty bucks that you're wrong."

Rudy gave an evil grin. "You're on."

He surveyed the room, looking at the men who filed in. The funny thing was that he saw guys who looked thick, muscular, and pretty tough, but when they talked, they lisped and simpered. It wasn't ex-actly a turn-off. He thought maybe these big, nelly guys would be able to take him. Clovis turned on a neon sign that read, "Clothes Check."

Most of the men disrobed. Tosh whispered to Rudy, "It's optional for the tops."

Rudy decided he wanted to keep his clothes on. He watched as men stripped, revealing flat asses, bouncy big butts, and everything in between. A few were pretty well hung. He wondered if they were tops. He caught a glimpse of Tosh's ass as he took off his socks. The hole hung loosely, with grey lips and a hint of red peeking through the opening. Rudy's boner strained against the cloth of his jeans. He realized he would probably lose the bet.

The bell rang. Tosh climbed up into a sling, legs raised in the stirrups. Rudy stepped up, pushing another guy out of the way.

"Hey!" The man protested.

Tosh said, "He's got priority, Melvin. You're next. Promise."

Rudy nearly knocked over the stool. The Crisco can hit the floor and rolled away. He cursed under his breath. "I'll be right back."

Tosh wriggled. "Hurry up."

Rudy snatched the can and moved the stool out of the way.

Tosh said, "Yeah, skip the fisting. I can't wait to prove you wrong."

Rudy pulled out his cock, letting it flop onto Tosh's small, soft penis. Tosh gasped, and his eyes widened. "On second thought, maybe you should fist me a bit to warm me up."

Rudy glared at Tosh. "We had a bet. You said you could take it."

"Yeah, but, uh, that was before I saw how big it is."

Rudy said, "A bet's a bet, Tosh. What are we gonna do here?"

Tosh dipped his hand in the Crisco, made a fist, and shoved it in his ass. He fisted himself for a minute or so. "Just lubing up."

"Cheater." Rudy laughed, but he was groaning

inwardly. He expected Tosh to chicken out. But Tosh was opening up. His hole yawned bright red, and a rosebud of flesh appeared at the opening.

Tosh said, "Okay. You gotta lube up, too."

"Of course." Rudy rubbed the white, creamy shortening up the length of his shaft, greasing the pole and the head until they reflected the bright lights. He stepped forward, placing the head inside the opening. Shit. This was going to be too easy. Sure enough, Rudy's cock went right in. Tosh squirmed and let out a squeak, but then he calmed down. Rudy was astonished when his hips slammed into Tosh's flat little ass. It was like throwing a hot dog down a hallway. Okay, maybe more like shoving a salami into a produce bag. But it was loose and easy.

Tosh wrapped his legs around Rudy's waist, pulling him closer. "That's the way, Daddy. Just like that."

Rudy cut loose, fucking harder. Tosh shrieked like a little girl. "Yes! Oh god, Yes!"

"You like that, little faggot?"

Tosh nodded. He was so loose that Rudy could barely feel the walls of his rectum. This must be what average guys felt when fucking an experienced bottom. He sort of missed Doug's stretchy ass that could still clamp down and give him a ride. Tosh was a horse vagina. In fact, those grey pouty lips looked like a pussy. Each time he pulled, the lips held on gently, turning out. When he pushed back in, the lips followed until Tosh's hole looked like an ass again. When Rudy accidentally pulled out too hard, a red lump like a prickly pear or a sea slug followed his cock out. Rudy's eyes nearly fell out of his head.

Tosh said, "Whoopsy-doodle. Prolapse. Don't

worry, it doesn't hurt. Keep fucking me." But Rudy was grossed out. He lost his hard-on.

When Tosh saw his inside-out ass was a deal-breaker, he said. "Okay, where's my twenty bucks?" Rudy fished a bill from his wallet and left it on Tosh's chest. As he walked away, Tosh said, "Okay, Melvin. You're up."

Rudy sat at the bar, nursing a beer. A big, burly guy dressed like a lumberjack came up and sat beside him. His low, masculine voice matched his big body. "Name's Howie." He offered his hand. Rudy took it.

"Rudy."

"You top or bottom?"

"Top."

Howie nodded. "Yeah, me, too." He held up a greasy fist. "It's always the same guys. I saw Tosh latched onto you like a leech."

Rudy chuckled. "He was a handful." He thought about the red sea slug that came out of his ass and retched.

Howie gave a loud laugh. "First time?"

"Yeah."

Howie leaned forward. His hairy chest gave off a musky scent that was pure manliness. "Between you and me, I like it both ways."

It might have been Howie's smell, or maybe just his low voice, but Rudy felt his cock swell. Howie looked down and whistled. "Shit, that's as big as my fist."

Rudy nodded.

Howie said, "I'd sure like to try it."

Rudy sighed. "Are you loose enough?"

Howie said, "No, but that never stopped me. I've got a hungry hole. You look like a seven-course meal." He put his hand on Rudy's thigh. "Shit, that's big. Come on."

Howie grabbed Rudy's hand and tugged him to the back room with the hobby horses. They were alone. He unbuttoned his plaid shirt, revealing a mat of chest hair under his wife-beater. His arms were strong and hairy. His biceps bulged as he unbuttoned his pants. In his underwear was a decent-sized cock. Rudy felt a tinge of envy staring at it as Howie got naked down to his boots. It was about the same length as Rudy's and half as thick. Big by any standards but not oversized.

Howie leaned into the soft, angled bench, exposing his furry ass. He reached under the horse, taking a can of Crisco from a hidden shelf. He passed it back to Rudy. "You do the honors, sir."

Rudy's cock responded to the honorific. Howie was putting him in charge, and he liked it. Howie's hole was not a sagging pussy like Tosh's. As Rudy worked a glob of Crisco up inside with his right hand, the hole responded by loosening. Rudy put one right finger in, then two.

Howie said, "Go on, make a fist and punch it. I like it."

Rudy made a fist and held it against the hole. With great effort, he felt his knuckles sliding closer to the sphincter. His phalanges disappeared. Suddenly, he slipped in.

"Oh fuck, yes!" Howie pounded the hobby horse. He looked back over his shoulder, a huge grin on his face. "Now the other one!"

Rudy was astonished. He put his other fingers up against his wrist and slid his left hand in, joining the right. Howie pounded so hard that Rudy thought he might break the furniture.

"Should I stop?"

Howie breathed out hard. "No! Hold me open and stick your dick in."

Rudy opened his hands, retreating, so his fingers spread Howie open. He pressed his rigid cock between his hands. Howie's ass shined with a reflection from the dim lights.

"Jack off inside me!"

Rudy was astonished. He'd never realized that was an option. He put his right hand back in alongside his cock. He grasped it and stroked it while he fucked Howie.

"Oh, shit, that's so fucking good!" Howie looked back at Rudy. His eyes were glazed over, unfocused. His thick beard was soaked with sweat. When the big, burly lumberjack shook his head, a few stray beads of sweat flew off, hitting Rudy's abdomen. Howie reached back and rubbed Rudy's butt, pulling him closer.

Rudy grunted. That moment of contact sent a shiver through him. It caused his balls to tingle.

With his free hand, he held Howie's waist. His hand grazed the furry belly, and he felt a static crackle. The energy between them was intense. In short thrusts, Rudy fucked his hand inside the hole, feeling his cock throb with growing excitement.

With the agility of an acrobat, Howie pulled his knees forward and rotated until he was lying on his back, facing Rudy. His lips moved in silent words; his eyes fluttered. Rudy admired Howie's hairy chest and treasure trail. He let go of his cock and withdrew his hand, letting the soft flesh retract like shrink wrap over his cock.

Howie bucked his hips, repeatedly impaling himself on Rudy's thick pole. Wet, squelching noises filled the air. Rudy found Howie's rhythm and worked with it, fucking him deep and pulling out just enough to let the wind out. He saw a satisfying gape between the man's ass cheeks. He entered and exited with an ease he'd never imagined. His cock felt small as it pressed into the cavernous hole without resistance.

Howie's feet kicked the air violently as he succumbed to a paroxysm of pleasure. His head thrashed back and forth, sharp breaths escaping between his clenched teeth.

Rudy lifted Howie's waist and tugged, burying himself as deep as he could go. He felt the pressure of his cock against the deep end of Howie's rectum. He pounded, punching against Howie's bladder, until a thin stream of urine trickled from Howie's soft, bouncing cock.

Rudy said, "Do you like it when I fuck the piss out of you?"

Their eyes connected. Howie nodded; he was beyond words.

Rudy gave a wicked grin. "Good. That's my specialty."

Each time Rudy pounded Howie, an arc of urine streamed through the air, soaking the floor and the two men. Rudy fucked like that until Howie ran out of piss.

Yearning to debase the man in every way he could, Rudy spat on his face. Howie licked it from his lips.

Rudy wanted more. He took his balls and held them against the opening until he could slide them inside. Howie clamped down, holding the balls inside him. Rudy rutted and thrusted, keeping the balls buried inside. He felt an urge to pee.

"Shit."

Howie said, "What, man?"

Rudy said, "I gotta take a piss."

Howie arched one eyebrow. "Do it."

"Inside you?"

Howie nodded.

Relieved, Rudy relaxed the neck of his bladder and felt warm pee flow out. With nowhere to go in Howie's rectum, it pushed past into the colon like a deep piss enema.

Howie jerked his cock, which grew stiff. He said, "Oh yeah, fuck! Fill me with your piss!" Howie's hand was a blur; he jerked off like he was shaking a can of spray paint.

Rudy's dick hardened further. The tingling returned to his balls. If he withdrew them from Howie's hole, the piss would escape. The Crisco and urine mixed in a warm, slippery slush. It put Rudy over the edge.

"I'm gonna come."

Howie pounded his cock furiously. "Yeah, do it."

Rudy didn't have much choice. The throbbing in his balls traveled up the thick shaft, releasing loads of semen in Howie's hole. At the same time, Howie's cock exploded through his blurry fist, splattering cum everywhere.

To Rudy's surprise, Howie reached under the horse and removed a small bucket from the hidden shelf. "You're gonna need this."

Rudy retreated, holding the bucket below Howie's backside. As his balls popped out, a milky yellow brew gushed out. When the head of his cock came out, a steady flow emptied mostly into the bucket. The floor beneath them was a slippery mess of shortening mingled with Rudy's body fluids. Had he not given Rudy the bucket, it would have been much worse.

Loud moans emanated from the next room. Every sling was full, but not every horse had a rider. Howie hiked up his jeans, letting his pretty penis hang out. "I'm gonna go get me some ass now."

He watched in awe as Howie stepped up to a skinny old man in a sling and stuck his hand in him. The experience had been great, but he was overwhelmed. He drove home, reliving the moment he cut loose and pissed up Howie's ass.

## ❧ 6 ❧

## TURNABOUT

Rudy dreaded getting back in the chopper with Doug. He'd heard that you're never supposed to fuck where you work; now he knew why. He didn't have deep feelings for Married Mike, but Doug, the porn star known as Ho Lee, had been an obsession for him even before they fucked. Sitting beside him, trying to gather the news, was like torture. They were polite to one another, like acquaintances, but Rudy wanted more. He was a starving dog looking through the glass window at a butcher shop.

Finally, one night, as they were wrapping up coverage of a traffic collision assignment, he couldn't help himself. "Doug, I know you said no strings. I just wondered if that was a one-and-done deal."

Doug rolled his eyes and hesitated. "I'll tell you what. We can hook up again, but this time, I'm on top."

Rudy's face fell in terror. "Y-you what? I'm a top."

Doug sighed. "Works every time."

Rudy had seen Doug's thin cock. He was desperate to hold onto what little he had with the man.

He stopped second-guessing himself. "Yeah, okay. I'm down to try it."

Doug said, "For real?"

Rudy nodded.

Doug shrugged. "Alright, you win. Your place, after this."

When they got back to Rudy's, Doug was all business. "Drop your pants; let's see what I'm working with. As Rudy tugged his jeans over his bulbous ass, Doug whistled.

"Damn! I was so busy looking at the engine up front that I never noticed the caboose! Choo Choo, motherfucker."

Rudy blushed. He was struggling to relax into the passive role. He didn't like Doug objectifying him. It made him feel weak, like he was less than a man.

Rudy said, "Can you cut it out? I'm not used to this."

Doug laughed. "Big top man's scared to play bottom, eh? You're going to be begging for it in a few minutes. Trust me."

Doug's dick got long when it hardened, but it didn't get much thicker. It was a little more than two fingers. Rudy sized it up, unsure if he was ready for it. He'd tried to put a carrot up his butt one time, and it hurt so bad he gave up. Doug was not a lot thicker than a carrot, at least.

"Bend over. I'm going to eat your ass."

Doug's tongue felt great. Rudy felt himself get hard involuntarily. Shivers ran through him, making him shake his head like a wet dog.

Doug pulled out. "You like that? Feels good, right?"

Rudy nodded. Doug spat into the hole, working

the slippery saliva past his sphincter with his tongue and lips. Rudy thought, "If it feels this good, maybe it won't hurt." Doug got up and excused himself.

Rudy said, "What're you doing?"

Doug tossed Rudy the Crisco. "Here, get good and greasy." He had already taken a glob for himself and slicked up his long, thin dick.

Rudy didn't like the way Doug bossed him around, but he figured that was how most guys had acted when they fucked him. He was just playing a role. Rudy didn't like his part. He wanted more control. It was moving too fast. But he wanted to snare Doug in whatever way he could. It was humiliating.

"Get up on the bed, face down. Yeah, like that. Now lower your ass."

Rudy complied. Doug slipped a finger inside.

"Ow! Slow down."

"Ow! Slow down." Doug mocked him. "Shut up, you big baby!"

Rudy was furious now. He was about to call it off when Doug bent his finger, pressing against the prostate. Rudy had no idea why it felt so good. Doug kept tapping it, milking him, until his huge fat dick started to ooze pre-cum.

"You like that?"

Rudy groaned. It felt great. Then Doug stuck in a second finger. He saw stars. Pounding the pillow, he said, "Fuck! Motherfuck!"

Doug laughed. "I took your whole fist, you dumb bitch. This is nothing."

Rudy realized he was in some sick power ritual, like a hazing. Doug was forcing him to submit to him, taking away all his power. It sucked. But when two fingers pressed that button, he didn't give a shit. He heaved a loud, satisfied sigh.

"Yeah, you like that, don't you?" Doug was still power-tripping. Rudy wondered if all that fucking Doug endured had caused some sort of rage to build up inside. It was anything but romantic. He'd never been cruel to any of his tricks. Of course, he never actually fucked any of them except Doug. Was Doug mad because Rudy was so big? Then the fingers pressed, and all his worries subsided.

"You ready?"

Rudy wasn't. "Yeah."

Doug pressed the tip against Rudy's slick hole and pushed. Rudy involuntarily clamped down hard, but he was slippery; he couldn't stop the invasion. The small head was inside. As Doug pressed, the dick slipped up Rudy's shitter. It felt creepy, like a snake wriggling its way inside. In a smooth glide, Doug bumped up against Rudy's back wall. He held Rudy's left hip and lifted it, then his cock went deeper, crossing an entry into his colon. Rudy gasped.

"Yeah, I'll bet you never knew that was there." Doug gloated. "You're too short and thick to get this far."

Rudy quivered. The violation was absolute. Doug was balls deep now, and Rudy couldn't stop him. His ass was too slippery to push him out.

"Relax, dude. It's easier if you just let it happen."

Rudy whimpered. He hated feeling dominated. Doug pulled back until he popped out of the colon, then slammed back in. He repeated it, each thrust growing a little less painful, until suddenly it felt okay.

"Now you like it, right?"

Rudy nodded, embarrassed by how good it felt. Doug fucked with an expertise only a bottom could muster. He'd been fucked by so many guys; he knew what felt good. Rudy didn't know it, but he was getting a high-quality fuck.

Doug put both hands on Rudy's waist, pressing him down towards the bed so his legs had to spread apart. His thick cock lay on the bedspread, drooling. Doug made sure to hit the prostate as much as he could with his thin dick.

Something snapped. Rudy let go of all his inhibitions at once. His animal urges took over.

Doug said, "You ready?"

Rudy said, "Fuck me."

Doug cut loose, fucking him hard and deep. The thin cock no longer caused him any pain. He was engulfed in a bubble of pleasure.

"Turn around, I wanna see your face." He held Rudy's thighs and rotated him, flipping him on his back. He pressed until Rudy's knees were by his ears. He fucked hard, smiling each time Rudy sucked air between his teeth.

"Bet you didn't know it felt this good."

Rudy said, "Shut up and fuck me!"

Doug laughed. "Horny little slut." He playfully slapped Rudy's face.

Each time the shame tried to rear its head, a wave of pleasure knocked it over and washed it out to sea. Rudy didn't care what it said about him or his manliness; this was a piece of heaven. His fat cock lolled on his stomach, drooling juice like a giant clam. Doug put his hand over it and rubbed.

Rudy jumped. "Oh shit, I might come."

Doug said, "I ain't stopping, so you'd better hold it." He let go of the thick dick, which throbbed and threatened to blow. Doug picked up speed until his hips were a blur.

"Your dick is a monster, Rudy. It's fucking beautiful. Oh shit, Oh, shit. It's turning me on so bad."

Rudy wrapped his legs around Doug's waist, giving in to the wonderful invasion. He didn't care if he was getting fucked like a bitch. It felt too good. Doug's cock popped in and out of that second, deeper hole, making a little noise each time.

Doug said, "I'm close. Are you?"

Rudy nodded. Doug pushed his belly into Rudy's cock, massaging it with each thrust of his hips. It gurgled and throbbed. Before he could stop it, Rudy blew a thick load onto his belly.

Doug howled. "Yeah, baby! Fuck that's so big! Oh fuck. I'm gonna come. I'm coming."

Deep in his bowels, Rudy felt a warm flood of semen. Doug slowed, then stopped. His cock softened and fell from Rudy's hole. A little trickle of cum stained the bedspread.

Doug stood and put on his underwear. "Do you have any coffee?"

Rudy frowned. "Will you stay with me?"

Doug frowned back. "I told you, dude, this isn't that kind of sex. I'm not your lover. We're just fucking. I got a guy already."

Angry tears welled up. Rudy let Doug turn him into a goddamn woman. His bitch. Now that the sex was over, he felt needy.

Doug wasn't the giving type. He said, "You know, skip the coffee. I'm beat. See you tomorrow."

Alone on his bed, Rudy got angrier. Fuck Doug.

He was a shithead. At least Rudy had something new to add to his repertoire. In fact, he was probably going to have to bottom a lot more. He didn't like the impersonal sex at the fisting club. He wanted a lover, one like Doug had. He never guessed that it was in front of him all along.

## ❧ 7 ❧

# YORK-HAWK

Rudy limped to the kitchen to put away the Crisco. He decided to sleep off the sex.

The next morning was his day off. He prepared to do laundry, emptying his pockets. He pulled out the phone number Doug had given him for York-Hawk, the porno company. He didn't hesitate.

"York-Hawk, Linda speaking. How may I direct your call?"

Rudy said, "Uh, yeah, hi. Um, a friend gave me this number, said to call."

After a long pause, Linda said, "Do you have a little more for me to work with?"

Rudy stumbled. "Yeah, I mean, I got a LOT more. Oh, haha. Right. My friend said this was how I could get into gay porno."

"Certainly. Would you like to come in for an audition? We take all types, just no fatties or femmes."

Rudy said, "Oh, I'm not fat or queeny. I mean, I'm fat down there. Oh, sorry. Was that too much?"

"It sounds like you might be a good fit. Pun intended." Linda gave him the details.

Rudy asked, "Is there a dress code?"

Linda tittered. "Just something that comes off easily."

The drive to the far end of the San Fernando Valley is always about 45 minutes longer than you think it will be. Luckily, Rudy knew this, so he left two hours before his audition, arriving in time to pick up a coffee and donut at Winchell's. The sugar and caffeine didn't help calm his nerves.

The studio was a sound stage built inside a warehouse in an industrial park. Linda, the receptionist and producer's assistant, was a thin, busty black woman with a kind smile. Her orange lipstick leaped off of her face as she spoke.

"Mr. Acker. Have a seat." Her eyes darted downward to the bulge in Rudy's gray sweatpants. She gave an approving smile. "Yes, you do seem like a good fit. But that's Donovan's decision."

After signing a release and completing some paperwork, Rudy flipped through the glossy magazines on the coffee table. This was no dentist's office. He was surprised by how many types of gay men were gathered in groups. There were big, furry, macho guys; slender, hairless, boyish men; men so black they were purple. It was a smorgasbord of gay sexual appetites. He flipped through "Macho." It was furry guys like Howie getting it on. He didn't see guys like Wolfe with fat cocks. They were all a little bigger than average, but not much. It was just regular dicks.

He picked up the "Big Winners" magazine. This was probably where he belonged. It was big cocks and stretchy asses. There was one guy who wore a Zorro mask. He had a mustache and a broad, furry chest. There was a tattoo of a lion on his left upper arm. His cock was long and thick, with a nice bush. He was taking it up the ass from a guy with way too much dick. The expression on his face wasn't hard to discern under his mask. His lips were curled in anguish. But a flip of the page and his grin told the rest of the story. Rudy didn't think he could stand something that big, but he knew what the grin conveyed. He had bottomed and liked it.

The producer, Donovan, opened his office door. He was older, out of shape, with grey temples. "Linda, who we got here?"

"This is Rudy. He doesn't have a porn name yet."

Donovan whistled. "Damn, that's one big chunk of meat you got there, kid."

He ushered Rudy into his "office," which doubled as a set. There was a big desk. Pointed at it were a still camera mounted on a tripod and a pair of teeny mole lights. The office was hot and bright.

"Here, let's stand you over there. He positioned Rudy in front of the desk. "Nice. Okay, hang on." Donovan held up a slate with "Rudy Test" scrawled on removable white paper tape and snapped a photo.

Rudy said, "Should I..." he gestured.

"Yeah, get naked for me. Ease up, relax. Pretend you're at home, waiting for a hot date."

Rudy removed his t-shirt, stepped out of his sweats, then pulled off his underwear.

"Holy Smokes!" Donovan stamped out his cigarette in an overflowing ashtray. "That's a hole-destroyer. Wow. Beautiful."

Rudy liked the attention.

Donovan said, "Get it hard for me, yeah?"

Rudy held it and gave it a good shake. He thought about Doug's loose ass. It didn't take much.

His cock swelled and lifted off his hand, pointing skyward.

"Oh, Jesus. That's fucking beautiful." Donovan snapped a few photos. "You're pure 'Big Winner' material. I can make you a star."

Rudy smiled proudly. Donovan snapped a few more shots. "That smile! Rudy! We gotta get you a porn name. Let me think about it for a bit."

Rudy dressed. He was curious. "When do I start? I have a pretty demanding job."

"With a dick like that, we'll schedule you any time that works."

## ❧ 8 ❧

## THE SHOOT

On his next day off, Rudy drove to Chatsworth to the weird little sound stage in the industrial park. It was sandwiched between ironworks, chop shops, and auto parts distribution centers. He saw a mechanic, on break, eating a breakfast sandwich and staring at Rudy with a hostile glare.

"Faggot."

Rudy bristled. "Yeah. So?"

The guy shrugged and went back to his morning meal. Fucking loser.

Rudy's first shoot was an office scene. Linda doubled as Wardrobe Supervisor. She had a dark blue perma-prest suit for Rudy, a starched white button-down, and a wide paisley tie.

She said, "No underwear, you dig?"

Rudy nodded and put on the businessman's uniform. His soft cock bulged in the suit.

"Sorry, sorry, I'm late!" A thin, short, cherubic youth rushed into the office out of breath.

"Hi, Ashton Smalls." He shook Rudy's hand.

"Rudy."

Donovan tutted. "Ah ah ah. We use porn names on set. I came up with yours. You're Stretch Buchholz."

Linda let out a laugh, then clapped. "Oh damn, that's good."

When Ashton disrobed to put on his suit, Rudy saw how he got his name. His penis was no bigger than a thimble, but his ass was huge. It was beautiful. His waist size must have been 26, but his ass probably forced him to wear 30.

Ashton stole hungry, nervous glances at Rudy's fly area.

"Is that as big as I think it is?"

Rudy said, "Probably bigger." He was relieved to be in a workspace where his colossal cock was openly celebrated.

Donovan sat back while two camera operators set up. One was a 16mm movie camera. Rudy hadn't realized he was going to be in a movie, but it excited him. Ashton's big ass added to the excitement. His trousers tented.

"Whoa there!" Donovan chuckled. "We need to see it soft. I guess we can pick up at the end."

The porn shoot was disjointed. There were frequent interruptions to move cameras or lights. It began with Rudy's cock already out, throbbing. Ashton knelt and took the tip in his mouth, struggling. He really sold it.

Rudy asked, "Is this a silent movie?"

Donovan said, "We do foley after the rushes come back. You know, dubbed grunts and moans."

Rudy grew up in Los Angeles, but Hollywood and its Valley counterpart were a mystery still. He was learning a lot of cinematic techniques, terms, and tricks.

After the oral farce, it was time for anal. Ashton lay legs-up on the desk. Rudy had to cheat to the side so they could get a profile of his hard dick against Ashton's puckered hole. The still camera clicked and snapped. They used a strange cream lube that didn't reflect in the lights and made his dick appear dry.

The film cameras were off for twenty minutes while Ashton struggled to take Rudy, but the still cameras clicked away. Once he was in, he had to pull out and pretend it was an easy entry for the first time. Ashton was a great actor. He pounded the desk, cried, and hollered. Then, as if it hadn't ever hurt, he smiled, holding Ashton close. They fucked for seven minutes until the 16mm camera ran out of film and had to be reloaded.

While they waited, Ashton said, "You must not get a lot of takers. I'm a pro, and that shit hurts like hell. You are the thickest guy I've ever seen."

Rudy nodded. "You're a trooper. Thanks."

Ashton smiled coyly. "No, thank you. This is going to make everything else seem like a cakewalk."

They fucked another seven minutes, then another, and more and more from various angles. Rudy's dick felt raw; Ashton was struggling to convey pleasure. They were worn out.

Donovan said, "Okay, time for the money shot, and then we'll do pickups of Stretch and his softie.

Movie cameras were off while Rudy jacked off. Ashton held his gaping ass open to motivate Rudy. When he was close, the cameras rolled. Following Donovan's orders, he stuck his cock in Ashton's hole, fucked for about a minute; then, when he was just about to blow, he pulled it out and sprayed cum all over Ashton's face. Rudy left his cock out while Ashton pinched his tiny cock between thumb and forefinger and stroked for a minute or two.

"Okay," Ashton said.

As the two cameras clicked and rolled, a massive load of sperm pumped out of his tiny balls, hitting his face, then chest, mingling with the puddles of Rudy's cum on his belly and chest. Seeing Ashton's giant load, Rudy swelled up again.

"Perfect. Back to initial set up." Donovan helped move the lights while Linda toweled off Rudy and Ashton. Their hair was sweaty, which didn't match the oral scene, so she used a blow dryer to restore continuity. Rudy's hardon subsided, thankfully.

Ashton entered the screen with a file folder and recited his one line.

"Sir, I have the Harden file. Where do you want me to put it?"

Rudy didn't answer; he just rubbed his hand on his fly. Ashton's jaw dropped in mock surprise. Rudy unzipped. Ashton pulled the plump, soft cock out of Rudy's pants, gasping. He knelt, putting the soft meat in his mouth long enough to get Rudy hard.

"Cut! That's a wrap!"

Rudy's cock throbbed as he changed back into his civilian clothes. He struggled to stuff it in.

"Great work today, Stretch." Donovan playfully patted Rudy's ass, then handed him enough cash to pay his rent and buy his groceries for a month.

## ❧ 9 ❧

# TONY

With his sore cock throbbing, Rudy drifted off into a very long sleep. The phone woke him up.

"Yeah?"

It was Tony. "Rudy, I gotta get you up to Pyramid Lake. Drowning."

Rudy checked his watch. He'd slept fifteen hours! "Oh, okay. Do I need to wait for Doug?"

Tony said, "He's off. We're short-handed, so I'm going to do the reporting."

This was a first. Rudy had never been in the same room as Tony, let alone a chopper. The producer was waiting for him when he got to the Tech Center. Rudy wore a worried expression on his face. It was never easy having to perform for your boss.

Tony smiled, climbing into the chopper. "I don't bite. Get in."

Rudy noticed Tony's arms for the first time. They bulged under his white Oxford shirt. The top of his collar sprouted thick fur. Rudy hadn't liked chest hair before, but it looked good on Tony. Once they were airborne, they chatted.

The producer said, "How long you been flying for us?"

"Uh, eight years, give or take.

"When was the last time you got a raise?"

Rudy smiled. "I don't think I've ever gotten a raise. You pay me okay."

Tony scratched his head and put a knuckle to his lips. "You're way overdue. Let's talk the next time you're in the office."

Rudy laughed. "The last time I was in the office was when I signed my employment papers."

Tony said, "Really? That's not good. We need to see your handsome face more often."

Was Tony flirting with him? He turned and looked at his boss. He wore aviator sunglasses on top of his head. He saw now that Tony had bright green eyes. They looked good against his deep tan. How had he never noticed Tony before? Maybe it was because he was his boss, and you're not supposed to think that way. But it was something different in Rudy, too. It was like that manly, macho energy was a turn-on now that he had bottomed for Doug. No, that was ridiculous. But it was uncanny. His cock started to throb. He rolled his eyes and sighed.

"Oh, no."

Tony said, "What?"

Rudy hadn't meant to say it out loud. "Uh, I just remembered I haven't paid my Water and Power bill, and it's due tomorrow."

Tony said, "Stay focused, Rudy. I don't want to crash in Los Padres Forest; they'll never find us."

The playful rebuke only made it worse. Tony wore cheap cologne, maybe Aqua Velva, which barely disguised the manly scent from under his arms.

Stay focused. Breathe. Think about macaroni and cheese. Think about your grandmother's bridge club. Anything, just focus!

Tony turned to him. "You okay there, brother? You're sweating."

Rudy smiled, pretending he didn't have a raging hard-on in his jeans. "I'm fine. We're almost there."

Tony said, "It looks like you're well on the way." He pointed at Rudy's lap with his eyes.

Rudy turned crimson. This was his boss!

"Yeah, I guess you caught me."

Tony rubbed his leg. "Thinking about Doug? He's got a big hole—big enough for you."

Rudy shook his head.

"No? Oh. Are you thinking about me?"

Rudy nodded. He glanced at Tony's lap and gasped. There was a long, thick lump down his left leg. It throbbed beneath the fabric. Thankfully, they arrived on the scene. Rudy's discomfort faded as they focused on capturing footage and Tony's live reporting.

There were two ambulances, two sheriff cars, and a highway patrol car for good measure. Several stretchers covered with white sheets dotted the shoreline.

Tony reported the tragedy in a deep, mournful, soothing voice. "Apparently two speed boats collided during a water skiing accident. There are several injured survivors, and the CHP is reporting four casualties."

The sun was setting. Rudy turned on the searchlight to better light the scene. They were the first chopper on the scene, but slowly, police and other television stations arrived until the air filled with endless clatter.

They wrapped up and headed back to the heliport. Tony wore a hungry expression as he stared at Rudy's package.

"I'm just gonna come out and say it. You wanna fuck?"

Rudy spit out his water. "What?"

"Never mind. That was inappropriate. Sorry."

Rudy said, "No. I mean, yes. Yes. I do." He couldn't believe he said that! What happened to 'Never fuck where you work'? Was he making a terrible mistake? His hormones were raging, and he just didn't give a shit. Fuck it. At least he could try.

They went to Tony's place, which was a big craftsman home up a steep hill in Echo Park, an old neighborhood with a severe gang problem.

Tony said, "Gangsters don't like to climb; it's safe up here."

"Yeah, but do the bullets climb hills?"

Tony said, "So far, so good. We formed a neighborhood watch. The cops are right down the hill at the Academy."

It was true; the palm-lined street was quiet. There was a spectacular view of downtown.

Tony pointed out a big, three-story house. "Tom of Finland lives there. He just moved in."

"Tom of Who?"

Tony said, "You don't get out much, do you?"

Rudy blushed.

His boss continued, "You ever seen those drawings of guys in black leather who are hung like horses?"

Rudy brightened. "Oh, like in the porno mags?"

Tony nodded. "He'd love you. He's already drawn me. I'm his type." To emphasize, he grabbed his crotch. It was swollen and long. "He'd love you. I can tell. He might add a few inches in length, but you look thick enough to pass the test.

All the chit-chat had distracted Rudy; his hardon had subsided. But the dick talk brought it back.

Inside, Tony asked Rudy to take a shower. "I go deep. You'll need to clean out. There's a nozzle."

Oh, no! Rudy realized that he might be in over his head when Tony tugged off his pants. His cock came free and slapped his thigh just above his knee. It was plump, thick as a wrist,

"Uh, Tony, I'm not sure I can take that."

Tony shrugged. "I'm an expert, don't worry."

Rudy resisted. "I'm a top. I've only ever been fucked once."

Tony said, "And how's that working out for you?"

Rudy admitted, "It sucks. I hardly get any." He didn't want to talk about his budding porn career with his boss.

Tony said, "Go with the flow. I promise you won't regret it."

Tony showed Rudy how to use the nozzle in the shower. It was pretty gross. He always thought the top did all the work, and the bottom just had to lie back and take it. He hadn't realized how uncomfortable it was to prepare for the act. Why hadn't Doug needed to do it?

Tony must have read his thoughts. "Your bottoms probably don't need to do this. I doubt you turn the corner."

It was true. The few times he'd fucked, it only

went to the end. It didn't go in that second hole at all.

After the third rinse, Rudy started to enjoy it. He liked the attention from Tony. His cock had shrunk at first because it was painful. When the pain subsided, he liked the sensation of being too full, then releasing. It was a new sexual experience for him.

Rudy toweled off and joined Tony in his bedroom. The curtains blocked out much of the light, but he could still see Tony's handsome face with its mustache adorning his upper lip. When he smiled, it was so sexy, Rudy's cock throbbed.

Tony marveled at Rudy's unbelievably thick cock. "It's a masterpiece."

Rudy said, "It's too thick."

Tony put his mouth on the tip, then widened, letting in another half-inch. Then, like a snake, he unhinged his jaw. With a surprised gasp, Rudy watched him swallow the head and keep going. He'd never felt anything quite like it. Tony's uvula tickled the tip until the majority filled his mouth.

Rudy said, "How did you do that?"

Tony grunted. His tongue was trapped, so he bobbed his head up and down. His mouth encircled the beast, as round as a painted clown at a bean bag toss. His eyes watered. He stopped.

"Damn, Rudy, I've sucked more than my fair share, and that's the thickest dick I've ever seen."

Rudy said, "You're the first one to get past the head."

Tony's face grew serious. "Now it's your turn."

Rudy blanched. "I don't know how to suck dick."

Tony laughed. "Well, then, we can skip the formalities and get down to fucking."

The boss man lay on his back, cock pointed sky-ward. "Hand me that tub of Vaseline." Tony slicked up his cock, then handed the tub to Rudy. "Work it in real good. You're gonna need it."

Rudy obeyed, marveling at Tony's thick pecs and silver-dollar nipples surrounded by a perfect patch of chest hair. He gasped when Tony turned, and his arm caught the light. There was a Lion Tattoo! Tony was the guy in "Big Winners" that he saw in the office! He thought he recognized that cock. He was going to say something, but they were about to get down.

Tony's nipple stood at full attention, just like his prick; it looked like the tip of a pinky. It was thick and stood out a half-inch.

"Okay, let yourself down nice and slow. Stop when it hurts, but don't back up."

Rudy stood over the long, thick, uncut cock. The foreskin had pulled down, so the head was fully ex-posed. Rudy squatted until the fat head touched his sphincter. He sat a little further, enough to get the tip just inside the hole. A blinding pain forced him to stop. He wanted to give up, but Tony held his waist firmly.

"Stay right there until it stops hurting."

After about thirty seconds, the pain subsided. He was afraid to keep going.

"I don't know if I can take it."

Tony handed him a glass vial wrapped in cloth netting. "Crush this and take a whiff."

Rudy was puzzled, but he did as he was told. In a few seconds, his head throbbed, and he felt all his muscles relax.

Rudy forced another half-inch before he had to stop. He waited.

"Sniff it again."

This time, it took a minute or more before he felt better. His ass was still sore from Doug, but for some reason, it didn't add to the pain. If anything, it made it more bearable. And the poppers were helping.

He let gravity force him lower. Another whiff of the poppers and the corona pushed past. Rudy saw stars. He waited, but now that he was on the slightly thinner shaft, it only took a few seconds.

Tony said, "It's smooth sailing now, at least for a while." He released his hold on Rudy's waist, which caused him to drop about five inches, stopping when the head hit the back wall.

Rudy shivered, wondering why it felt so much better than Doug. His ass was stuffed. He realized the girth of Tony's cock was enough to apply constant pressure on the prostate. Clear juice dribbled from the head of Rudy's cock.

Tony said, "Okay, let's just ride that for a while. Do you want to stay standing?"

Rudy shook his head. Tony deftly took him by the waist and pushed him onto his back, never letting the head of his cock fall out. When Rudy was settled, Tony pushed the shaft back inside. As the head moved forward, the pressure on Rudy's prostate subsided slightly, then grew as the thick middle of Tony's cock pressed it. The intense pleasure forced a sigh.

Tony said, "Does it hurt?"

Rudy shook his head. "It feels beautiful."

Tony agreed. "Best feeling in the world."

The boss dragged his head back and forth, pressing and releasing the gland, milking Rudy's cock. He put a finger on Rudy's cock head and dipped into the sweet juice, licking his finger.

"You taste good."

Rudy was surprised. He'd never tried it. He took a finger full and tasted. It was like a salty syrup. His cock hardened.

"I'm gonna speed up now. Okay?"

Rudy nodded. He watched the long cock disappear and then reappear at an ever faster rate. It was so long that Rudy could still see half the shaft exposed. He remembered Doug turning that corner. Tony was so much thicker. Would it hurt? Probably.

After a few minutes of good, strong fucking, Tony paused.

"You know about the second hole, right?"

"Yeah."

Tony said, "Okay. Let me go there."

"Do it." Rudy was scared, but he wanted Tony inside him all the way. He took a whiff of the poppers.

Tony lifted Rudy's left hip. Gently but firmly, he pressed against the inner door until it opened. With a loud pop, the head passed through.

Rudy trembled. "Oh, fuck."

Tony pressed forward. "Does it hurt?"

"Nah, it's not that bad."

Tony slapped Rudy's ass. "Not bad? Just wait, it'll feel fucking great." He slapped his ass again, pulling out past the inner hole. In time with his exit and entry into the colon, he spanked Rudy, causing him to let go. He still had a few inches to go but worked on loosening Rudy up first.

It still hurt a lot, so Rudy sniffed the poppers.

Suddenly, it felt a lot better. And it kept getting better.

"Oh, shit, Tony. That feels so fucking good."

Tony smiled. He stopped slapping Rudy's ass and took longer strokes. Rudy fell into a deeper and deeper hole that overwhelmed his senses. Tony was an expert fucker. He took a long outstroke, his head squeezing Rudy's prostate, then went straight in until his pubic hair tickled Rudy's backside. Then he pushed another inch, and his pubic bone rested on Rudy's cheeks.

"You like that?"

Rudy couldn't respond. His neck relaxed, and his eyes rolled. He was in ecstasy.

"I'll take that as a yes." And then Tony proceeded to fuck the hell out of him. In long, fast strokes, he went from tip to base, slamming his hips hard against Rudy's ass. Each time he passed the inner hole, it made a loud snap.

Rudy felt a strange wave building in his gut. It was like the pleasant release when taking a shit, but over and over. In waves, the pleasure built until he began to spasm. His cock throbbed.

"Oh fuck yeah, you're one of those." Tony stopped fucking, letting Rudy's involuntary contractions massage his cock until they subsided. A few more strokes, and they started up again. Tony kept at it. Each time, the spasms grew more powerful.

"You're gonna make me come, Rudy."

Just hearing those words set off a chain reaction in Rudy. His balls churned, and his cock spat a thick load of gyzym onto his belly and chest.

Tony pounded the bed, "That was so fucking hot. Oh, oh, you're making me come!"

A warm flood filled Rudy's guts. Tony's manly sweat fell in droplets, soaking Rudy's face. The big man collapsed on top of him, getting Rudy's cum in his belly hair.

Tony stayed buried, letting his cock soften. It was too thick and long for Rudy to push it out. He didn't care. He wanted Tony to stay there forever.

After a few minutes, Tony withdrew. His greasy, cummy cock hit the bed. Rudy knew his ass was gaping wide. A fart escaped in a soft sigh.

Tony laughed. "You won't hear them for a week."

SMALL-TOWN BOY AND TONY

## ❧ 10 ❧

# LEO LONG

I n the kitchen, Rudy helped Tony prepare a
spaghetti dinner. He shifted from foot to foot,
his ass throbbing. He wondered if he'd have to
eat standing up.

After dinner, Tony said, "You'll get your turn
tomorrow."

Tomorrow? Rudy was surprised. "You mean this
isn't a one-time thing?"

Tony frowned. "Did you want a one-and-done? I
thought we had something special just now."

Rudy nodded excitedly. "No, it's just that I
haven't found a guy that wanted to stick around."

Tony said, "Fuck that. You're a keeper."

Rudy needed to clarify something. "Did you
mean that I get to fuck you tomorrow?"

Tony nodded.

"I'm too big. Are you sure?"

Tony said, "It's only fair. I've been fucked a lot
more than you. I was only your second. I figure it
won't be much harder than what you did. I'll keep
the poppers close."

Rudy had another question. He hesitated, then

took the plunge. "I take it you're familiar with that magazine 'Big Winners?'"

Tony stopped short. "Yeah, very."

Rudy said, "Me, too. Yesterday, I got very familiar with it, too."

They both laughed. They were a couple of porn stars.

Tony said, "I'm Leo Long. How about you?"

"Stretch Buchholz."

That put Tony into a fit of laughter, the kind where you gasp for air and tears form in the corners of your eyes. It was contagious. They held each other, laughing.

Tony said, "Oh no, I can't breathe."

"Me neither!"

Eventually, the giggles subsided.

Tony dropped Rudy off at his car. He shifted uncomfortably on the ride home. Tony had fucked him silly. It had been incredible; he was excited to return the favor.

# II

# FRYING CHICKEN

The following evening, Tony came to Rudy's house. When Rudy answered the door, Tony had his cock out. It barely fit through the fly. Rudy could never do that. They didn't make zippers wide enough!

The sight of Tony's semi-hard cock caused Rudy's beast to swell.

Tony held up a fresh tub of Crisco. "I won't chicken out."

Rudy remembered his mother frying chicken in Crisco. He laughed. He liked how comfortable he felt with Tony. It was so different from Doug's cold demeanor. Being close to a man who wanted to be with him was new to him. Their eyes met. In an instant, they were kissing. Tony shed his coat and unbuttoned his shirt, tugging the bottom hem from his pants. It fell open, exposing his beautiful, soft fur and huge nipples.

In a gentle tug, Tony pulled Rudy to his chest. Like a hungry infant, Rudy put a big nipple in his mouth and sucked. Tony quivered. "Oh fuck, that's good." His cock swelled and rose off his pant leg. Rudy wrapped his palm around it, his fingers not quite touching. In long strokes, he jerked off his boss.

When Tony put his hands on Rudy's shoulders, he didn't have to push. Rudy knelt, placing the tip of the big cock on his tongue. He opened wide, accepting the head into his mouth. He pressed forward until the cock filled his mouth, still swelling until it was trapped behind his teeth. When the head reached the back of Rudy's throat, he gagged. When he tried to remove it, he couldn't. It had swelled to its full size.

Tony put his hand over Rudy's and showed him how to run it up and down the long shaft. Rudy's panic subsided. He jerked the shaft and sucked the head. He knew the rhythm a man likes when he's jerking off, and he did it perfectly. As long as he kept just the head in his mouth, he didn't gag. He sucked and swirled his tongue over the head, determined to bring Tony to orgasm. It was all new to him, but his instincts were perfect.

"Man, you're good. Oh, right there, just like that."

Rudy's steady strokes and determined tongue teased that salty syrup from Tony's fat cock. With his free hand, he reached up and pinched a nipple. Tony shuddered.

"Oh, fuck! I think I'm gonna come. Oh, man."

Rudy didn't change his pace. He jerked long and fast, feeling Tony's skin slide under his fingers.

Tony gasped. "Oh, oh, oh! Right there! Oh, here I come!"

Rudy choked down the salty brew as it spurted out. Tony held Rudy's ears and fucked his face. Rudy gagged, spitting up some of the cum so it came out of his nose. It burned. Despite the discomfort, Rudy liked the way Tony dominated him and forced him to worship the big, beautiful cock.

After a minute, Tony began to go soft. Rudy pulled back, catching a few drops of cum in his palm. He slurped it up, savoring the strange flavor. He swore it was so strong it made his chest hair grow.

Tony excused himself, holding up a bulb syringe. "I gotta clean out again. That was so good, I nearly shit my pants!"

In Rudy's bedroom, Tony said, "I think you're gonna have to use your hand to warm me up. You ever fisted?"

Rudy felt proud when he said, "Yep. A few times."

"Good. I'll need it."

Rudy's finger slipped in without protest, so he added two more and flexed, stretching the hole a little wider. Tony didn't complain. Soon, Rudy had four fingers and added his thumb.

"You can stay right there; don't go all the way yet."

Rudy collapsed his fist to form a cone, pressing his fingers to his thumb. He pushed in and out, working his way closer to his knuckles each time. After about three minutes, the widest part of his hand bumped up against the muscle.

Tony cracked a popper and inhaled deeply. "Go. Now."

Rudy pushed hard and slipped in. The ring stretched, then clamped down around his wrist. He relaxed his fingers, finding the prostate and pressing gently. Tony came out of his amyl nitrite haze.

"That's it. Oh, yeah." Rudy pushed in, curling his fingers as they reached the end of the rectum so the top of his forearm could enter. He pulled back, feeling his tightened fist trapped behind the ring. He formed the cone again and pulled until his hand snapped out.

"Ow, shit! You gotta warn me."

Rudy said, "Sorry, boss."

"Don't sweat it. Hang on." Tony pressed against one nostril and inhaled with the other. A few seconds passed. "Okay, now."

Rudy pushed back in, this time feeling less resistance.

"I'm coming back out."

Tony nodded and inhaled in the other nostril. "Okay."

Whoosh! Rudy's hand slipped in. He kept it up until Tony no longer needed the poppers.

"Okay, Rudy, go in, but make a fist on the way out. On my cue."

Another whiff of poppers. "Now."

Rudy pulled his tight fist out, watching in awe as the hole gaped open, exposing a bright pink tunnel.

"Okay, make a fist and go back in."

Rudy punched the hole, sliding in with relative ease.

Tony let out a shriek. "You gotta wait until I'm ready." He sniffed. "Okay, out."

They did the dance until Tony gave the go-ahead. "You can punch fuck me now. Go as fast as you want."

Rudy felt powerful as he punched and pulled,

forcing his boss's hole to open wide and stay there before snapping shut.

"You can go faster."

Rudy obeyed. The squelching sound sounded like bubbles at the La Brea Tar pits. Pop-pop-squish, he was destroying Tony's hole.

"Stop. I'm ready now."

Following the lead he'd gotten from Tony the day before, Rudy lay on the bed, greasing his cock with shortening.

Tony knelt over him, adding more Crisco to his loose, pouty hole. Rudy's cock was at least five inches shorter than Tony's.

Tony pressed the head against his asshole and bent his knees slightly, letting the tip in.

"Fuck, Rudy, your dick is bigger than your fist."

Rudy was tired of hearing it, but now that he'd been the bottom, he felt sympathy instead of frustration.

"You can change your mind."

Tony shook his head vehemently. "No way. I've wanted this ever since I hired you."

Rudy let that sink in. Had he gotten the job because of the bulge in his pants? Probably. Did it matter? Not really.

His mind snapped to attention when Tony bore down, letting another half-inch into his hole.

"Ow, fuck!" Tony broke open another glass vial. After a few seconds, he sat down hard. The head popped in, and the whole length of Rudy's shaft filled his hole. He shuddered violently, then relaxed.

Tony shifted until his feet were out from under him. He bounced up and down off Rudy's hips.

Tony said, "God, that feels good."

Rudy knew he was pressing the joy button really hard with his morbidly obese cock. Tony's balls smacked Rudy's. They were heavy. Next to the man's long, thick cock, they appeared a lot smaller, but they were actually massive. Tony's cock was completely soft. Rudy picked up Tony's heavy balls and massaged them. He watched the big cock puff up.

Tony took Rudy by the wrist and placed one hand on his nipple. Rudy pinched and twisted, causing Tony to shiver. His teeth clacked together as he rode the fat monster. He bent over and kissed Rudy hard. Their tongues found each other and danced.

Tony was a big guy. Like a wrestler, he grabbed Rudy and rolled until the pilot was on top.

Rudy's instincts took over. His hips thrust; his cock pounded the back of Tony's rectum.

After a minute or two, Tony hissed between his teeth. "Rudy, I think I'm gonna pee the bed."

Rudy picked up the pace. "I'm gonna fuck the piss out of you." And he did.

Rudy was powerful. He submitted to his boss yesterday, but he was in control today.

Tony whimpered and moaned. "Yes! Just like that."

Rudy didn't need instructions. His body knew what to do. Air began to escape Tony's hole in loud farts. Rudy liked it.

"Yeah, I'm fucking the farts out of you, too."

Tony laughed. Rudy realized how funny it sounded. He joined in. Fucking through laughter was challenging but joyful. He put a hand on Tony's chest, brushing against his nipple as he stroked the silky hair. Tony bucked.

"Please, please squeeze it," Tony said.

Rudy obliged. Tony's cock lifted off his belly until it pressed against Rudy's chest. It drooled. Rudy arched his neck and took the tip, tasting the nectar as he swirled his tongue on the fat head.

Tony groaned. "Oh fuck, you're gonna make me come. Not yet. Not yet."

Rudy straightened his neck. The head stayed pressed against his chest. Tony was rock-hard. So was Rudy.

He wished he could turn the corner, but he wasn't long enough, and even if he were, he would probably rip Tony in two trying to get there. He didn't care right now. His cock was in heaven right where it was. And it was getting closer to nirvana. He could feel his slippery pre-cum mixing with the Crisco, making Tony's flesh highway slick. Slippery when wet.

Tony wrapped his legs around Rudy's waist and tugged Him closer. Rudy began taking shorter strokes, which brought him another step closer to coming.

The friction of Tony's cock against Rudy's chest must have been what caused him to shout, "Oh, fuck, I'm gonna come again!"

Sure enough, a thick load hit Rudy on the chin and cascaded down onto Tony's face. He licked it up as best he could.

Seeing that was the last straw. Rudy felt the familiar gurgle as his cock swelled, ready to spit. Then it came. In long waves, Rudy pumped his semen into his boss's ass. There was nowhere for it to go. With loud slurping sounds, it squirted backward, out of Tony's ass, and onto Rudy's thighs. With one final thrust, he shoved his cock in, causing Tony to hit the headboard. Then he collapsed on top of him, their lips locked in a passionate kiss. Rudy's soft, heavy cock fell out of Tony's gaping hole with a wet slurping sound. They stayed in a tight embrace until they drifted off to sleep.

# THE KISS

The alarm went off at 4:30 am, giving Rudy just enough time to shower, dress, and get to the chopper for the morning commute.

Tony was already on Rudy's phone, barking orders at the news writers. He put a hand over the receiver. "I still need a shower."

Rudy said, "No sweat, just lock the door on your way out."

The chopper blades thumped as Gina reported the tie-ups and smash-ups on the never-ending LA freeways. Rudy's mind was on Tony. He yearned to be with him again. He'd felt this sort of longing before, but never for a guy who wanted him back.

His heart skipped a beat when he landed the chopper and saw Tony waiting.

Gina said, "Oh, what's he doing here?" She studied Tony's expression, then smacked Rudy's arm. "You've been holding out on me. You're diddling the boss!"

Rudy blushed and stammered. "W-No! I mean— how did you...I mean yeah, okay. You got me."

Gina hugged him. "Oh god, please don't fuck it up. Tony is such a bully when he's single."

Rudy waved at his boss. The cat was out of the bag. He couldn't hide it, then realized he didn't want to. He walked right up to Tony and kissed him. Tony didn't flinch. They wrapped their arms around each other, letting a warm, comforting joy spread between them. Rudy's cock stirred.

Tony said, "Oh, is that what I think it is?"

Rudy said, "Mmhmm."

"Well, let's go take care of it."

# EPILOGUE

The common wisdom against workplace romances is usually pretty solid, but not in the case of Rudy Acker and Tony Cazzone. They started as steady fuck buddies, but there was too much love in the air. Tony owned the big house on Laveta Terrace. He convinced Rudy to stop paying rent, and they shacked up. Their relationship grew more intense, spiced with the flaming hot sex that left them both gaping and satisfied. As word of the hot couple got out, Donovan called them in for a few films. Leo Long and Stretch Buchholz were big porn stars. They didn't even need the money, so they used it for lavish holidays.

They enjoyed a camaraderie that men with big dicks know well. Tongues wagged when they walked down the streets of Mykonos or Ibiza, displaying their packages in Brazilian swimsuits, putting on a show for passersby. Why try to hide what they were given at birth?

Rudy caught the eye of his neighbor, Touko, better known as Tom of Finland. He spent time in Tom's garden, letting the artist photograph him. It was amazing to see his face and cock brought to life in comics and lithographs. Tony had been right; Tom added a few inches to the length, just as he'd plumped up Tony's cock a little.

Rudy's life until he met Tony had been an empty husk. He knew there were missing pieces. He awoke when he allowed himself to be penetrated. He thrived when he let another man love him and gave love in return. Accepting and feeling proud of his massive dick was another missing puzzle piece that helped bring him to wholeness.

Like most gay relationships, there was an incubation period when the two remained exclusive. Over time, the relationship opened up, allowing outsiders to join them in the bedroom and even in films. When they searched for a third, Tony was better at spotting the bottomless bottoms that could handle a pair like them. As their sexual conquests expanded, legends sprang up about the porn couple who modeled for Tom of Finland and whose cocks could split a man in two. They live there still in Echo Park. Their unsanctioned love has outlasted most marriages.

# DUTCH TREAT

by Adam Maxwell Bigglesworth

# DUTCH TREAT

I flew a jumbo jet from Los Angeles to Amsterdam overnight. By law, I wasn't allowed to fly an airplane again for another 14 hours. Even though the airline would pay for it, I had no desire to leave the airport to find a place to sleep, as I would have to return through customs and immigration. The Pilots' lounge was cramped and not very private, so I opted for a mini-hotel inside Schiphol Airport within the sterile zone, requiring no immigration or customs to return. It was a threadbare place, mostly for tourists. Each room had a small bed and a television with bad reception. The showers were shared. The hotel was divided into men's and women's sides. The men's side reminded me of a bathhouse, only cleaner.

I'm not a big guy. I'm 5'5", skinny, with a well-below-average penis. Okay, a tiny penis. Being small has kept me from enjoying sex. I feel inadequate, so I rarely engage. The obsession with my small size has also turned into an obsession with big cocks. Just seeing one makes me hard, not that anyone could tell. I'm neither a grower nor a shower.

So, with that lack of self-confidence, I wrapped my waist in the small towel they provided and headed to shower off the grime of a ten-hour overnight flight. The showers were shallow stalls without curtains. I was relieved to see I was alone when I started my shower. I hated other men to see my little penis. I lathered up my hair with the all-purpose soap, closing my eyes to keep it from burning my eyes. I was very tired, so I kept my eyes closed under the shower, opening my mouth to let the warm water in, and enjoying the sensation as it pelted my skin.

I opened my eyes when I heard the shower directly across from me turn on. There were a dozen showers, and this guy picked the only one that invaded my privacy. I kept my back turned, afraid the man would see my little dick.

"Hey, guy. How's it hanging?" The voice was a deep, rich, Texas drawl.

I glanced over my shoulder. "Okay, I guess. And you?"

"You're a California boy, ain'tcha?"

I was annoyed at the onslaught of questions, but I answered. "Yeah, I guess it sounds like I have an accent to you. Texas, right?"

"Yep. The Big D."

"Dallas. I've flown there a few times."

"Just flew? Didn't stay?" The Texan was relentless. I liked his low voice, though. It made my skin tingle in a good way.

"I'm a pilot. I don't usually stay over after short flights like that."

The Texan crossed a line. "You gonna keep

showing me your ass, or are you gonna turn around and talk face-to-face? Not that your ass isn't pretty or nothing."

I groaned. I didn't want him to see my small penis. He'd never say anything, I figured, but it would be humiliating all the same. I shrugged and turned to face him. Between his legs was the biggest dick I had ever seen.

He whistled. "Oh, damn, that's small."

Adding to my shame, the sight of his cock gave me an instant erection.

"Yeah, I know it's small. Sorry."

"Don't apologize, son. I like the little ones best of all."

I took a moment to look at the rest of his body. He was maybe six feet tall. His green eyes sat above ruddy cheeks and a handlebar mustache resembling something from an old Western. His muscled chest was covered with a light dusting of hair. His farmer's tan made his arms look even bigger than they were. And that colossus between his leg was lifting off of his thigh.

"Take a picture, it'll last longer."

I blushed. In truth, I'd probably jack off to a picture like that if I had one. "Sorry, man, I, uh..."

"Never seen a dick this big? Don't worry, I'm used to it."

I realized, reviewing our conversation, that he said he liked little dicks. Was he gay like me? His throbbing cock grew even bigger, answering my question for me. He licked his lips and grinned.

"I got a bottle of Jack back in the room. You wanna join me for a drink?"

I said, "I can't drink. I'm flying soon."

The Texan chuckled. "Yeah, but do you wanna come join me?" He rubbed his stiff cock as he spoke. "It looks like you do." He gestured with his eyes to my crotch.

My cock was so hard, it bounced up and down as the blood pulsed through it. I had trimmed my pubes recently, and it was way more obvious than I expected. He licked his lips a second time, rubbing his mustache. He winked.

"I'm in room 17. Knock twice."

He couldn't be bothered to hide his appendage as he wrapped the towel around his waist and then left the shower. I dried off, my head spinning. What would I do with a guy like him? I was so out of practice I'd probably split in two. And there was no way that cock would fit in my mouth. It was as big around as a can of corn and twice as long. But I wanted to see it again. It would give me another entry in my spank bank, if nothing else. I'm sure he'd let me touch it, stroke it, worship it. Beyond that, I doubted I could do much of anything. "Fuck it," I thought, "let's see what happens."

He answered the door completely naked. His cock was drooling pre-cum like a faucet. He said nothing, pulling me into the room and planting his lips on mine. We explored each other's mouths and let our hands roam across our bodies. His butt was a muscular bubble of flesh. His hands found my ass.

He pulled away and said, "Oh man, that's a perfect ass."

"I was going to say the same."

He smiled and pulled me close, so his massive

cock rubbed against my little thumb-sized dick. We moved to the small single cot. He grabbed a bottle of baby oil from the nightstand before laying on his back, his cock towering high above him.

He said, "You can try and suck it if you want, but it's not much use. It won't fit."

He was right. I licked the head like an ice cream cone, but he pulled it away and upended the bottle of oil, letting it cascade down the glans and shaft.

"Go on and rub that for me. Get it good and greasy."

I obeyed. He stretched and moaned while I stroked him.

"Damn, boy, your little fingers feel good on my big dick."

I blushed. I hated my small hands. They barely fit around the flight controls. I couldn't get both sets of fingers around his monster cock. It was massive beyond belief.

He said, "You're getting pretty wet down there."

I glanced down and saw that my little pecker was dripping. I was so turned on by the huge cock in front of me I hadn't noticed.

He reached and caught a bit of my flow in his huge palm and licked it. "Sweet. Bring it here."

I shifted so he could plant his mouth on my cock. He licked it like a clit, swirling it on his tongue. It was all too much for me too fast. I trembled.

"Oh shit, I think I'm gonna cum."

He said nothing, just buried his nose in my pubic hair and licked harder. My head began to swim, and I felt my little ball sac pull up. I shivered as I came in his mouth. He lapped it up like a thirsty dog. He kept licking until I had to pull away because it was too sensitive.

He patted my ass. "Wish I could have some of that."

I smiled. "We could try."

He held his cock, slick with baby oil, and pointed it straight up. I climbed onto the bed. He lowered the angle so I didn't have to stand on tiptoe to get the head near my ass. I have a really big ass, and the hole is a little bigger, too. I was clearly built to be a bottom. I wasn't so sure the Texan was built to be a top. He'd need to be a little smaller to get much play.

As I positioned my ass over his cock, I stumbled. I didn't fall, but I landed on his cock, and the head popped in. I saw stars. The pain was excruciating. I tried to pull off, but I was at a bad angle. I began to slide down until the Texan caught me by the ass and held me there.

"Slow down, son. You're gonna split in two!"

I wanted him to lift me off, but his arms wouldn't reach. I managed to get back on my feet and rose up a little. There was no relief from the pain. His hands still held my ass. He lowered me gently. I felt the head push forward until it reached the back of my rectum, where it pressed against my bladder. My legs quaked. I groaned in pain.

"We can stop. I can see it's too much."

I said, "I didn't go through all that just to give up."

I was maybe halfway down the shaft. Half was still exposed to the air. I didn't think we could go any deeper, but he tipped me to one side, and with another powerful blast of pain, I felt him invade my colon. With the worst part over, I sat down in his lap. The outline of his cock head bulged in my belly. He was as big as a man's arm. I had never been fisted, but it must feel like this. The pain had gone from 11 to 4. I wasn't comfortable, but it was bearable.

In a swift motion, he rolled until I was on my back, and he hovered above me missionary style.

"You ready to rock and roll?"

I wasn't, but I nodded.

"Here I come."

He withdrew halfway, enough for the head to pop out of my colon, then plunged back in. I shook from the sudden jolt of pain. He repeated this slow fuck several times until I felt a wave of relaxation wash over me. The pain diminished, replaced by a growing wave of ecstasy.

"Oh fuck, that's good."

He nodded. "Good for me, too."

After a dozen more slow fucks, he picked up speed. Each thrust came a little sooner than the last until he was smacking into me hard. It should have hurt, but the endorphins had kicked in, and I was high with lust. My eyes glazed over.

The Texan said, "Glassy eyes. You're ready."

"Ready for what?"

He didn't answer. His rapid thrusts accelerated until his ass was a blur. A loud clapping sound deep inside my bowels got louder and faster until it sounded like an audience after a command performance. My skinny legs kicked involuntarily. I swooned in and out of consciousness as my insides quivered. My abdomen convulsed involuntarily as a new sensation washed over me. I was shaking with an orgasm, but no cum was coming out. It wasn't the same kind of orgasm. It didn't stop; it just grew more and more as he pounded me hard and fast.

A bead of sweat trickled down his forehead, off his nose, and into my open mouth. It tasted like a man. I convulsed harder.

"You're one of them. The guys who come inside. Why didn't you tell me?"

I struggled to say, "I didn't know."

"First time with a big guy?"

Between gasps, I said, "You're. Not. Big. You're. Huge."

He laughed. "It takes me a long time. You good with that?"

I felt like I was a contestant in the sexual equivalent of a pie-eating contest. The fucking was good, but a long time sounded like too much. I shook my head.

"I can stop." He slowed down. The convulsions stopped. I needed them. I needed him to fuck me.

"Don't stop! Fuck me!"

He needed no further prompting. He pounded hard and fast again, and the waves of ecstasy poured over me. I wrapped my legs around his waist. He kissed me, his tongue invading my mouth like his cock invading my insides.

The kiss was powerful. I felt a tingling in my balls that signaled another round of cum was ready. My eyes fluttered, and then I shot my load against his belly.

"Did you just come again?"

I nodded, my tongue pushing back and digging into his mouth. His mustache tickled my nose until I nearly sneezed. I convulsed, and the ass orgasm went into high gear.

I turned and saw myself in the floor-length mirror. The cock looked as thick as my leg from that angle. I got hard again, just watching myself as if I were watching a porno in a dirty movie theater. Only I hadn't seen a dick this big, even in the movies. He made John Holmes look like a regular guy.

The oil was wearing off, and the friction started to burn. The Texan pulled out. I felt air blowing in my gaping cavernous hole. He quickly dribbled more oil on his monster and shoved it back in, sliding easily past my rectum and into my colon. I couldn't have resisted even if I wanted to. I was an open tunnel and his train was charging ahead like the TGV.

He put his hands behind my back and lifted me until he was in a standing position with me straddling his waist. His hands slipped under my bottom, and he began bouncing me like we were playing ride-a-horsey. He walked around the tiny room, resting me against the wall for a spell, then moving on. I bumped my head against the wall-mounted television set. It turned on, blaring the news in Dutch. He reached up and turned it off, not missing a beat. He was so far up inside me that I pictured him coming until it blasted out of my mouth.

He grunted. "Oh, shit, you're good. I'm close."

I breathed a sigh of relief. "Oh, man, come inside me!"

"I said, 'close', not 'there'."

What did close mean? Was it another 30 minutes or 30 seconds? He put me back on the bed face down, holding my hands behind my back, thrusting so hard my head smacked into the wall. He pulled on my arms to stop the head banging. I didn't care. I was convulsing again, and my balls were tingling.

He said, "It feels good when you twitch like that."

I couldn't speak, so I groaned in agreement. Then I felt my balls pull up again. "I'm gonna come again."

He said, "You didn't even touch yourself. Oh fuck, that's hot. I'm there, too."

"Come inside me, fill me up."

The clapping sounds were deafening as he thrust harder, faster, and deeper than ever. His strokes grew longer. I pounded the mattress, overcome with orgasm.

He lifted me wheelbarrow style. "I wanna see that little dick come."

He got his wish. I shot a huge load on the blanket. Then I felt him shake.

"Oh, fuck, son, that's hot. Here it comes."

He ground his pubic mound into my ass cheeks, buried deep, and let loose a flood of pent-up cum. I could feel his cock throb, and his testicles squirmed against my legs.

"Aaargh! Oh fuck! Oh, sweet Jesus." The flood continued, warming my insides. Buried inside me, he rotated me to face him and lifted me to his lips. We kissed passionately, locked together by the huge cock buried in my guts.

The kiss caused my little penis to harden again. He felt it press on his belly. "You hard again?"

I shrugged. Then I felt his softening cock switch directions until it was rock hard inside me.

"The second time takes a lot longer."

THE NEXT MORNING, I limped as I walked down the gangway. Jeannie, a stewardess friend, asked if I was okay.

"Yeah, but I'm gonna need a pillow to sit on during the flight."

# ABOUT THE AUTHORS

**Peter Schutes** is the nom de plume of a prolific and acclaimed novelist. As Peter Schutes, he is the author of Adult Erotic Fiction such as <u>The Slaves of Rome</u>, <u>Dark as a Dungeon</u>, <u>The Gospel of Priapus</u>, and <u>Panama Heat</u>. He writes in the style of vintage pulp authors from the 1960s and 1970s. He lives in Los Angeles.

**Adam Maxwell Bigglesworth** is the pen name of an aristocratic one-time heir to the throne of Scotland and a literary novelist.
Adam is the author of many novellas and short stories, including Chopper Jock and Satan's Sissy Boy. Although his family lives in the Midlands of England, his roots are on the Isle of Lewis in the Outer Hebrides.

## OTHER BOOKS FROM PETER SCHUTES PUBLISHING

**E-books and Paperbacks**

The Able Seaman

The Anaconda Copper

The Autobiography of Peter Schutes

Backwoods Delivery

Big Bodies of All Sizes

Big Hole River

Bobbing Buoys and Salty Seamen

Bunkhouse Buddies

The Butt Baby

Chopper Jock

Cloistered

Confessions of a Rodeo Clown

Dark as a Dungeon

Demonic Deception *aka* Deceived, Cursed & Blessed

Desert Island Daddies

Dirty Dorms and Fresh Men

Dutch Treat

The Expectant Member

Firehouse Lovers

The Fish

Five Erotic Tales

The Gospel of Priapus

Hercules and Lippos
Hobo Honey
Hot Blue Collars
Hotshot
Logger's Delight
Muscle Bottom
Panama Heat
Satanic Seductions
Satan's Sissy Boy
The Slaves of Rome
The Thigh Baby
Under the Boardwalk
World's Biggest

***** Coming Soon *****
Like the Greeks Do
Hoboes, Hustlers, and Jailbirds
Tales of Two Daddies
More Tales of Two Daddies

www.ingramcontent.com/pod-product-compliance
Lightning Source LLC
Chambersburg PA
CBHW011152310726

48973CB00010B/2871